TORN

TORN

DAVID MASSEY

Chicken House
SCHOLASTIC INC.
NEW YORK

Text copyright © 2013 by David Massey

All rights reserved. Published by Chicken House, an imprint of Scholastic Inc., *Publishers since 1920*. CHICKEN HOUSE, SCHOLASTIC, and associated logos are trademarks and/or registered trademarks of Scholastic Inc.
www.scholastic.com

First published in the United Kingdom in 2012
by Chicken House, 2 Palmer Street, Frome, Somerset BA11 1DS.
www.doublecluck.com

No part of this publication may be reproduced, stored in a retrieval system, or transmitted in any form or by any means, electronic, mechanical, photocopying, recording, or otherwise, without written permission of the publisher. For information regarding permission, write to Scholastic Inc., Attention: Permissions Department, 557 Broadway, New York, NY 10012.

Library of Congress Cataloging-in-Publication Data

Massey, David (David Robert), 1960–
Torn / David Massey. — 1st American ed.
p. cm.
Summary: Only nineteen when she is sent to Afghanistan, British army medic Elinor Nielson is continually at odds with her hard-nosed bunkmate, Heidi Larson, but connects with a mysterious Afghan girl and local children, as well as an American lieutenant.
ISBN 978-0-545-49645-2
1. Afghan War, 2001 — Juvenile fiction. [1. Afghan War, 2001 — Fiction. 2. Soldiers — Fiction. 3. War — Fiction. 4. Medical care — Fiction. 5. Afghanistan — Fiction.] I. Title.

PZ7.M423823Tor 2013
[Fic] — dc23

2012024405

10 9 8 7 6 5 4 3 2 1 13 14 15 16 17

Printed in the U.S.A. 23
First American edition, August 2013

The text type was set in Chaparral Pro.

Book design by Nina Goffi

For Bob and Maggie,

and for all those who have fallen in Afghanistan

1

FIVE A.M. I'M WOKEN BY YAPPING DOGS AND THE first distant call to prayer, carried to me on a light breeze. My first morning in Afghanistan.

Private Elinor Nielson, recently qualified medic, first tour of active duty. That's what I keep telling myself — over and over like a demented idiot — to calm my nerves. *I'm just a normal nineteen-year-old English girl . . .* Of the hard-core, life-saving variety, that is. What a laugh. I'm like the love child of House M.D. and Lara Croft.

Today, for the first time, I'll be going out on patrol here — with an SA80 assault rifle in one hand and hemorrhage-stopping supplies in the other. Can I really do it? I have to remind myself that I'm doing something with my life, that I'm going to help people. It's why I joined up.

But the reality of it all still hits me as I lie in my canvas bunk. Real blood. There will be real blood, real pain, real casualties depending on me. Not some squaddie pretending. *Don't think about it*, I tell myself. My new mantra. In fact, not thinking may be the best way for a medic to stay sane out here.

I haven't had much sleep — and not just because of the nerves. Note to self — go to bed in thermals rather than underwear. After the stifling heat yesterday when I arrived, I didn't realize that the nights would be so cold. And the changing temperature made the bunk's metal frame creak as it contracted. It's creaking again now, this time expanding as the sun rises. I wonder who slept in it last. Then I remember there was a "sudden need" for another medic in Helmand province . . . I decide not to ask my roommate about it.

She's Heidi Larson — another medic and a corporal — but is nowhere to be seen this morning. Her drying underwear and spare cargo pants hang from a red nylon rope between our bunks, acting as a kind of gappy camouflage screen. I wonder if she's done it for privacy. If so, it isn't working. I didn't need to see the stripes on the jacket sleeve to figure out that she outranks me. When I arrived, she looked down her precise, upturned nose at me like I'd crawled out from beneath a rock. I get the feeling that if we are ever to be friends it will only be after a firefight or one of us has nearly died.

I swing my legs off the bed, wrap myself tightly in a towel, and make my way through a corridor of huge wire-meshed blast bags to the open-air shower. It's in an unused corner of the base and is reserved for the use of the women. The wiry, ginger-haired squaddie who insisted on showing me to my bunk yesterday pointed it out, and I intend to make the most of it. Apparently the washrooms would normally be in converted freight containers but the base is still waiting to have them installed. When we're on ops, my guide told me, I'll have to stay dirty like the men or make do with a quick splash from our water bottles.

The shower is in the middle of a tiny courtyard surrounded by peeling whitewashed and windowless walls. Its green copper pipe sticks out above curtains made from a scummy gray tarpaulin suspended from the showerhead on a rusty hoop. I squeeze through the gap, pull the curtains together, and slip off my towel — only to discover that the tap is outside, on the wall. *Crap. Double crap.* I grab my towel, hold it loosely to my chest, and make a run for it. It takes two hands but when I turn the tap the pipe creaks and shudders, spitting out a yellow stream of what I think must be water.

After waiting for it to run clear I hurry back and chuck my towel over the curtain rail, trying not to scream when the cold water sucks all the heat from my body. As soon as I get used to it I lather my hair and close my eyes.

It is not until I throw back my head to squeeze the water from my hair that I realize two things — one, the shower is visible from the flat mud roof of the adjacent building, and two, there are three squaddies standing on it, looking right at me.

Whoops of laughter break out when they see they have been discovered.

As they disappear from sight over the roof, one of the pervs yells, “Thanks for the show, newbie!”

 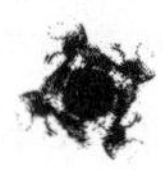 

Corporal Larson is in our room when I get back. She could be a model — tall and thin, with skin even a Hollywood star would kill for — and she’s all muscle. She has short hair — a crew cut — but the lucky cow could shave the lot off and still look amazing. Her gun is in pieces beside her on her bed as she cleans and oils it.

“I would have appreciated a warning about the shower, Corporal . . .” I say, throwing my towel on the bed and struggling into my fatigues.

She shrugs. “I forgot.”

“Thanks,” I mutter.

“You’re welcome.”

She might be past caring who looks at her body, but I’m not. I’ve never been the type of girl to play strip poker at a party or go topless on the beach.

Heidi clips her gun together while I sit on the end of the bed to put my boots on. There is a loud *click*. I turn to see her shouldering her weapon, her finger on the trigger. It’s aimed at the round mirror I've brought with me that stands on a pile of boxes by the wall. From where I sit, her head is framed in it.

Great. Just perfect. Trust me to end up bunking with a psycho.

It is a relief to escape to the noisy makeshift canteen for breakfast. My short hair dries almost completely on the walk over.

The main part of FOB — Forward Operating Base — Freeman is a large compound surrounded by a few one-story mud-brick buildings. They're all linked by corridors of blast bags like the one I walked through to get to the shower.

In the canteen I pick up a tray and stock it with juice, toast, and some disgusting goo labeled "strawberry porridge." As I scan the room for a seat, I see three guys sitting on their own, grinning at me. All are in their late teens or early twenties: a lad with sun-bleached hair and a cocky smile, a very good-looking black guy wearing headphones, and — stupid me — my ginger-haired guide from last night. My Peeping Toms.

Why did this have to happen on my first day? Inside, I'm dying. Why didn't I check the roof? What was I thinking?

Of course, there is an empty seat at their table. I look around for another, but can I find one? It's like the whole platoon has got here before me. It's my own fault. I took too long getting back from the shower. I couldn't turn the stupid tap off and all the time I was looking over my shoulder, paranoid the pervs were going to reappear. Just as I was about to give up, I realized you have to push the handle down while you twist.

The blond guy stands up and waves. "Over here! Nielson, isn't it?"

There is nowhere else for me to take my tray. I mouth my complete stock of swearwords at the floor and decide that the best form of defense is attack. Smiling, I make my way over to them, lifting my head and looking right into the blond guy's eyes.

"So, you lot must be the camp jokers," I say.

Ginger pushes back the empty seat with his boot and grins at me like a Cheshire cat. He holds out his hand, which I am definitely not going to touch, and says, "I kept a seat for you. Remember me? The name's Yugi."

No wonder he was so keen to show me where the shower was. Hope they had a long, uncomfortable wait. I don't ask him to explain his nickname, even though I can tell that he is itching to tell me.

He does it anyway. "Cos I always keep a pack of cards stuffed up my sleeve — like in *Yu-Gi-Oh!*" Then he gets them out to show me, as if I don't know what a pack of cards looks like.

"I'm Gizmo," the black guy mumbles sheepishly, taking off his headphones.

"And everyone calls me Chip," Blond Guy says, then he smiles at me as if introductions mean everything is cool.

I smile back. "Short for chipolata?" I suggest.

Yugi almost chokes on his tea, Gizmo lets out a huge roar of laughter that has all eyes looking our way, and Chip flushes red.

I'm already regretting the joke. After all, I've got to work with these guys.

"Nice," Chip says, throwing his friends a dirty look, "but no, it's because I'm a mean poker player. Proper cards — unlike Yugi's."

"If you say so." I sit down with my tray.

"Hey, we'll need a nickname for you, if you're really going to be a part of the team," Yugi says. "Something shower-related. How about Buffy? You know, like *in the buff*?"

The others laugh.

"I'll tell you what." I'm so nervous I'm almost shaking, but I manage to keep it out of my voice as I tell them firmly, "You can call me Elinor, Ellie, or Nielson, but if any of you ever call me Buffy, you'll be going home singing soprano."

But they're still grinning. There's no point fighting it. I'm stuck with Buffy and, if I know soldiers, the nickname will have gone viral by the time breakfast is over.

Yugi leans into me. "By the way," he whispers, "nice tattoo."

"Yeah, good to meet you *in the flesh*," adds Chip, back on track.

I have a tattoo along the small of my back — a line of jagged flames quite low down so it won't stop me from wearing a backless wedding dress one day. (My two-timing ex was training to be a tattoo artist and needed practice.)

I can feel the color drain from my face. "You had binoculars?"

"The best, baby . . ." Chip draws a high-powered rifle scope from his pocket.

"I'm not your baby," I return, trying to keep it light even though his constant joking is already starting to annoy me.

"Just a bit of harmless fun, OK?" Chip holds up his hands in mock surrender, but he doesn't look that sorry.

I raise my eyebrows. "I'll remember that when you're screaming for a medic."

I think their stunned silence means they get my point.

2

MY FIRST PATROL IS RIGHT AFTER BREAKFAST. I'M told it's a routine one to a small village called Ghoray, a couple of miles from the camp. We only had ten minutes to get kitted up and into the compound. If it hadn't been for a heads-up from Gizmo as he left the canteen I would have been late for roll call.

Now I'm standing by the corrugated-iron gates of the base, loaded with so much gear that I'm panicking about whether I can make it a couple of meters let alone a couple of miles. Beyond the gates a dirt road cuts through an ancient-looking wild-olive grove on its way toward a range of blue-gray mountains that are stacked against the horizon. The outer walls of the base are tall, more blast bags piled on top of each other, but with spaces left for two huge machine-gun emplacements. The whole thing is topped with rings of razor wire.

I can't help fretting that there's something I've forgotten. The backpack pulls painfully on my shoulders like I'm giving my eight-year-old cousin a piggyback, and I could swear it almost weighs as much. We haven't taken a single step outside the gates yet and already I'm dripping with sweat. The heat is intense and, to top it all, the body armor weighs a ton, too. It's like wearing a gym mat. Smells just as rank. I feel sick.

Focus on the training. You can do this. At least, I know I could do this a whole lot better if only I could find somewhere quiet and take a pee. In the rush to get ready I ran out of time for a trip to the crapper — squaddie slang for the toilet. There's a row of them at the far side of the compound, leaning against the perimeter wall, mocking me. It's only a hundred meters or so but I don't want to ask to go now because I'll hold everyone up and look like a complete idiot.

Heidi is in charge of an advance team of eight of us, divided into two groups of four. I am teamed with Chip, Yugi, and Gizmo. The corporal smiles but her hazel eyes are cold when she gives them the news. *So even Heidi knows who my Peeping Toms were.* I do my best not to react.

"There is no law in Helmand," Gizmo tells me as we make our way toward the gates. "Every day we have to go out, to make the locals feel safe and to let the Taliban know they can't just come back and terrorize people. The minute we relax they are back out there planting IEDs."

Improvised explosive devices. *Don't think about it,* I tell myself. *Use the mantra.*

Near the gates are the machine-gun emplacements I spotted from the helicopter yesterday. I can't help but notice the pile of spent rounds to the right of the gun, hundreds of empty brass tubes glittering in the morning light. One of the gunners is clearing them up with a shovel. There's also a row of huge vehicles that are missing wheels or axles, bleeding oil.

"I thought the British Army had vehicles that were resistant to mines," I say to Gizmo when we pass them.

There's a snort of laughter from Yugi.

Gizmo indicates the wrecks with a sweep of his arm. "Ta-da! You're looking at them. MRAPs — Mine Resistant Ambush Protected vehicles."

"But how . . . ?"

"They were built to withstand last year's IEDs. *This year* the insurgents have doubled the amount of explosives they use."

"Do your sightseeing when we get back, Nielson," Heidi barks, glaring at me. "Get up front with Chip and keep your eyes peeled."

Chip gives her some unfathomable look, then leads the way through the gates and on to the road. He's carrying a black high-tech mine detector and wearing headphones. Our point man. He waves at us to be quiet and walks slowly, carefully scanning the ground in wide, arcing sweeps. The cockiness of the canteen has completely vanished. He's calm and deadly serious, professional. I'm right behind him, with Gizmo and Yugi following. With Heidi there's a serious, square-faced guy called Greg and a short guy with Asian features called Danny. Bringing up the rear is a guy with prematurely gray, marine-cut hair who is known to everyone as Jug. They tell me he is an Iraq veteran.

I try not to look fazed, even though my heart's thumping as we make our way in single file along the dirt road toward the olive grove. *I've had training*, I repeat to myself. *I want to fit in. I can do this.* Up close the wild olive trees are huge. Their wide trunks are like old, twisted rope, fraying at about head height into thick branches. Most of them seem to lean in the same direction, toward the distant mountains. When we are through it, we take a smaller road that I didn't see from the helicopter. It branches off into the lowlands. Either side of me there are wide patches of tall, scrubby grass that seem to merge into untidy clumps of stunted trees. Through the gaps I can see stretches of the dusty plain beyond. At least the ground here is quite flat. I might even make it a few miles before I collapse under the weight of my gear. With any luck we'll be stopping for a rest by then.

Yugi's seen me taking things in. "This part of Helmand is known as the Green Zone."

"I was expecting it to be all desert," I admit.

"Yeah? You're thinking of the safe bits. Out here you have to have eyes everywhere. And I mean everywhere. The Taliban hide in trees, irrigation ditches, houses, you name it. Hell, sometimes they don't even bother hiding."

Gizmo grunts. "Stop it, Yugi, you'll freak her out." Then, to me, "We're a team, Buffy. We'll watch your back."

I'm grateful for the reassurance and go back to scanning the ground. I know what I'm supposed to be looking for, in theory — telltale signs that it has been disturbed.

"You won't see anything," Gizmo adds, even though he's doing exactly the same thing. "The guys laying IEDs are experts. And the heat out here dries any mud to a crust in minutes. But look for patches that seem too smooth or unnatural. If you have a gut feeling that anything isn't right, trust it."

"Those mine detectors aren't much use anymore, either," Yugi says from behind me. "These days the Taliban are using wooden blocks rather than old-style metal contacts for the trip switch. And they're wrapping them with the thinnest fuse wire you've ever seen. Don't expect Chip to pick anything up with that piece of crap. Here all you have are these" — he taps the side of his eye socket — "and these" — he pulls at his earlobe.

"Thanks for the vote of confidence, mate, but I'd take this thing over your ears any day," Chip mutters over his shoulder, and Gizmo laughs.

After that I examine the gray dust at my feet like I can will my eyes to see through the ground. But no matter how hard I try, it all looks the same — sunbaked, cracked, treacherous.

The heat is like nothing I have ever known. It must be nearly ninety degrees and the sun isn't even at its highest point yet. It's so hot the sweat has dried to a tight crust on my face. Every now and again I use some of my precious water to wash it off.

Farther from the base, the dirt road becomes rougher, cutting through uneven ground, often obscured by short, unfamiliar trees. The fields on either side are scored with deep ditches and waterways, and I can't help but feel exposed. A target. Like Yugi said, there are too many places for someone to hide out here. I start to get that feeling that makes you want to look over your shoulder. A couple of times it even makes me shudder. I manage to block it out and hope the others haven't noticed my jitters. Every now and again we pass people on the road, mostly women wearing loose trousers beneath surprisingly colorful tunics, and long shawls. The women stop and wrap the shawls around their faces as we draw near, and they look over the hems at us with strange, dark expressions. I can't tell whether it's curiosity, hatred, or nothing at all. Maybe it's tension. After all, they could tread on an IED, too.

One woman is balancing a huge sack on her head. I whisper to Yugi when we've gone past her, "Where are they going?"

"God knows," he says unhelpfully. "Buying or selling stuff in other villages or taking food to their blokes in the fields. Around here, those that aren't Taliban are farmers."

About three hours' walk from the base we finally reach Ghoray — a one-road place where half the mud-straw houses are bombed-out skeletons. It should have taken half the time but we have to make constant stops to check patches of road that Chip thinks look suspicious. I thought that seeing civilization again would be a relief, but it's not. You could cut the tension with a knife. Heidi tells us to reassure any locals who will talk to us, and to scan for insurgents. It sounds straightforward. Routine.

Reassuring and scanning. OK. I can do that. It would be so much easier if I didn't look like the Terminator in all my kit though.

Before we enter the village we drop our packs and chug some water. I can't express the relief I feel as I slide out of the straps. It's like the world has been lifted from my shoulders and someone has turned on the air-conditioning. A light breeze cools my soaking back. I can see that the others feel the same, and we all stand there for a moment to dry our sweat-darkened combat jackets. To my relief I also notice a sheltered ditch where I can finally have my pee. Gizmo and Chip stand guard for me, out of sight. By the time I get back the shower thing is *so* forgotten.

Our break doesn't feel anywhere near long enough, but we have to get under way again. We walk on between the tree-lined walls and an irrigation ditch filled with slow-moving brown water. Now some of the locals smile as we pass, and I find myself suspicious of the reason. I've only been here a day and already the place is getting to me. It is impossible to tell whether the smiles are genuine, and whether the kids pointing their finger guns at us are playing or wishing they had a real one. Any of the Afghans we see leaning in openings or shadowy gangways could be holding a pair of wires and a battery, waiting for an unwary foot to fall on the right spot.

Out of the blue a woman's head pokes out of her window and she screams abuse at us. Heidi takes Greg and goes to talk to her. I hear Heidi trying to talk Pashto. While they are at it, an old guy gestures for us to follow him, and scrambling ahead of us up a slope he takes Chip, Gizmo, and me over piles of rubble to point out the wreck of what must once have been his home. It's just an untidy pile of bricks kept from tumbling any farther into his neighbor's property by a few stubborn knee-high walls. God knows where he is living now. Maybe he's with the madwoman whose shrill voice is still ringing behind us.

"Americans!" he keeps saying, holding out his hands and looking to the heavens. "Americans — BOOM!"

While Chip tries to calm him down, I ask Gizmo, "D'you think that's true?" He seems genuine. It's hard seeing what our bombs have done to normal people, to their lives.

Gizmo tells me, "You have to be careful. They know there is compensation if we've done it. All we can do is check it out."

Chip is trying to explain that the army will make it right if his story is true, but I don't think the guy understands English. In the end Heidi calls us on and we have to leave him standing there, staring at us as we leave.

I don't know why, but this last meeting has really freaked me out. I think it was seeing the guy's anger and frustration, knowing that he's still back there, blaming us for what happened. We march on and now every corner of the village seems to breathe a silent threat as we walk. It's impossible to tell whether the rubble we see everywhere has just fallen or been placed by careful hands. A tense, uneasy hush falls upon us and we continue in silence, scanning the black windows and broken walls with our weapons raised. A noisy group of sparrows flutters away at the sound of our approach. Even though I'm with my team I suddenly feel very alone. It's impossible to explain the feeling, but I know it's not just my imagination. We are definitely being watched now.

My heart is pounding in my ears. Every bit of me is on edge. Each time my boot touches the ground I expect something to happen.

The others sense it, too. Fanning out, we keep to what cover we can find. Heidi and her section fall farther and farther behind as their pace slows. Looking behind me, I notice her stopping to send Danny and Greg into some empty buildings and I think I should tell Gizmo, especially as the next few steps we take will take us round a bend in the road. Soon we'll lose sight of them completely. Gizmo is behind Chip and me, watching our backs, and Yugi is out on the flank at our right.

My heart flutters in my chest.

I've left it too late. When I look back again there's no sign that the others are still with us, and we have lost sight of

Heidi's section. I open my mouth to warn the guys that we need to wait for them to catch up. That's when it happens.

A loud metallic *click*.

Chip and Gizmo dive for cover against a low wall on the left side of the road and they squat there, scanning the wrecked buildings around us for the source of the noise. Me? Like a fool I just drop to the floor where I stand.

I locate Yugi, he's fine but he hasn't moved for cover or dropped to the ground like me. He seems rooted to the spot.

"Yugi!" I hiss, getting to my feet and making my way over to him.

He doesn't reply. He doesn't even look like he is breathing. His shoulders are barely moving. Then I see his face. It is white with terror and beads of sweat dribble out from under the rim of his helmet.

"*Get away from me.*" His voice is hoarse.

"What's wrong?" I'm confused.

Yugi's pupils are wide, locked onto mine. "Please just go," he begs, and a tear forms in his eye.

"I'm not going anywhere . . ." I begin.

"You two OK?" Now Gizmo is scrambling to his feet and making his way across the road toward us.

Suddenly Yugi's cheeks flush, and he yells, "GET THE #@*! AWAY FROM ME, ALL OF YOU!" He even starts to raise his gun, but I can see his arms are shaking.

Gizmo stops dead and tells me quietly, "Back off, Buffy. Do what he says."

I ignore him. "Yugi, you're scaring the crap out of me. What's going on?"

Yugi blinks back the sweat and tears, and his watery eyes meet mine. He whispers to me through trembling lips, "For God's sake, *Buffy*. I'm standing on an IED. If I move my foot, we're both going to die. Go away." Then he pauses and adds, *"Please?"*

Suddenly I'm finding it impossible to breathe. I have to help him to relax and the only way to achieve that is to do what he wants, at least for now. Maybe Chip or Gizmo will know how we can help him. "Wait there," I tell him, then, "sorry," as I realize what I've said. Yugi's hollow laugh follows me while I run over to Gizmo.

"Wassup?" Chip comes to join us.

"He's standing on an IED."

"Bloody hell . . ." Chip hesitates, then points his gun back to the corner of the derelict wall where a tall tree leans out over the road. "We'll need to take cover, then, and let Heidi know what's going on."

"No! We've got to get help."

"There's no time to wait for help," Gizmo tells me. "That thing could go off any moment."

"So we're just going to leave him there?"

"If you've got any ideas, Buffy, we're all ears," Chip snaps, his finger hovering over the radio "talk" button on his weapon. "Well?"

It turns out we don't have time for a debate.

Without warning, a stream of automatic rounds ricochet off the ground around us, sending up a scattering of small dust devils. We sprint back to the corner for cover.

"Welcome to Helmand, Buffy," Chip jokes when we get there, but his face is grim. "Looks like you're getting the red-carpet treatment." He takes a quick look over the wall and drops back down again. "I think it's coming from that low ridge — one o'clock. Cover me."

Gizmo swings his gun over the wall and lets off a few rounds in the general direction, while Chip scrambles around the corner and disappears from sight.

At the same moment Heidi's voice crackles in my headset, "Chip, what's happening?"

Gizmo presses the "talk" button on his rifle and tells her. "Sniper. And Yugi's on an IED."

There's an irate silence, then Heidi says, "We're on our way."

Whoever is firing stops, briefly. I'm feeling stupid, like I should have given Chip some covering fire, too. I look back at Yugi. Somehow he is still on his feet, but I can see that his legs are shaking. Any moment he's going to set the IED off and I wish, with all of my being, that I can come up with some way of helping him, but my mind is blank. My training was all about treating injuries, not defusing bombs. Then the shooting starts again and I realize something. Something important.

"Gizmo . . ."

"What?"

"He's not shooting at us."

"Don't be daft, Buffy. This is what happens here — they shoot at us and we shoot back. Now get ready to cover me. I'm going to help Chip flush him out."

"No, really." I hold him back and point as another rapid line of rounds blasts the ground by Yugi's feet. "He's trying to blow the IED."

3

THERE IS NO TIME FOR GIZMO TO RESPOND. Answering fire rattles from Chip's SA80 on the other side of the wall. It's a crisper, more controlled sound than the one from the sniper's gun, shorter blasts. Gizmo joins in for a second or two and I copy him, sliding my back up the wall until I can see over it.

The rubble-scattered ground slopes up toward a low, scrub-lined ridge. Chip is a few meters in front of us now, behind a tree. The sniper's position on the ridge is obvious — a small outcrop of rocks obscured by bushes. I aim at it and pull my trigger. I never expected my first firefight to feel like this, but it's . . . exhilarating. Like the gun is spitting out all my tension. The feeling worries me so I stop and drop back behind the wall.

Chip shouts, "Gizmo! Get your arse over here! He's moving position."

Before he leaves, Gizmo looks at me. He's noticed the way I keep checking on Yugi . . . He grabs my arm so I'll focus on him. "Don't do anything stupid. Promise?" He holds my gaze for a moment, clearly wondering if he can trust me to do as he says. "Look, the others will be here soon. We don't have to do this alone."

As if in answer, there is the crackle of gunfire behind us in the village. It looks like the rest of the platoon has troubles of its own.

Heidi's voice rattles in my ear again. "Gizmo, two shooters opened up on us just as we were moving out. We're pinned down — you'll have to manage without us for a while."

Over the wall, Chip lets off a few more rounds and yells, "GIZMO! NOW!"

Gizmo looks at me with the question in his eyes.

"OK!" I promise. But it's a lie.

I watch Gizmo's back until he disappears around the end of the wall, and then I turn my attention back to Yugi. He is standing as still as stone, but I can tell from the way his body shudders from time to time that he is struggling to hold his position. It is taking all his concentration to keep his foot still with the same pressure it had exerted at the moment it fell.

The sides of his fatigues are black with sweat. I'm wracking my brain when an odd memory of my gearhead dad, making one good VW Camper out of two wrecked ones, tugs at the back of it. He'd take me on regular trips to get useless parts weighed by scrap dealers, and he'd make a game of it on the way. If I could guess the weight, I'd get the money. I'm wondering . . . would it be possible to replace his foot with something that weighs the same without setting the detonator off?

"You OK?" I call.

"Been better," he whimpers.

I'm still thinking, hoping for something better, but there's nothing else there. Most times I would win the money. Most times . . .

I shout over, "I'm going to help!"

"Forget it, Buffy, I'm dead." Yugi tries a laugh. "I was hoping to get legless tonight, but not like this."

I look around. I can't see anything to use in the road, but there's a bombed-out building just behind Yugi. It's worth a shot. I slip off my backpack and leave the cover of the wall, making my way over the road at a crouching run.

The report of Chip's and Gizmo's weapons clatters off the buildings every now and again. And behind me Heidi's team is still shooting, too, answered by the heavier clack of the enemy's weapons. All the way I feel exposed, wondering if the shooter is going to open up on me, or if there is another IED detonator buried beneath my feet. Maybe all my efforts will end in instant and complete darkness, and I will never know if Yugi makes it.

When I get to the doorway, I'm breathless with effort and fear. Sweat and fatigue are making my eyelids heavy, and I have to squeeze them with my fingers. I raise my gun. The sodding barrel shakes. Pulling it tight against the strap helps a bit. I've only ever done this in training and with several guys as backup. By rights, I should chuck a grenade in, but I don't want the shockwave to trigger Yugi's IED.

"Come on, Nielson," I mutter to myself, and pull my elbows in, as if by doing so I will be able to squeeze away the nerves. Then I step inside.

The room is cool after the scorching heat of the road, but I can't enjoy it. I'm panicking too much because I can't see after the bright sunlight outside. It seems to take forever for my eyes to adjust. When they do it's a relief to see nothing but shadows and dusty piles of rubble, and an old door hanging from one rusty hinge. It is homemade from old planks and plywood — it's perfect. With a few kicks I knock out one of the splintered panels, then tip dusty armfuls of rubble onto it, about the weight of a man's leg.

There is another series of whizzing, reverberating shots.

I run to the doorway to see dust from the bullets showering Yugi's boots. It's a miracle the shooter hasn't hit the IED yet.

Yugi's eyes are closed and his lips are moving.

Gizmo and Chip return fire again, but they're more distant now. They must be following the sniper, herding him away from Yugi, making his task more difficult.

The incoming rounds stop. The sniper must be on the

move again. I'm not going to have much time before the shooting starts up again — and then he's bound to hit the target.

I look at my pile of rubble on the door panel, then cast a critical eye at Yugi's wiry legs before taking the decision to kick some of it off. A voice in my head reminds me of those times Dad managed to keep his money, but I shut it out. Then I drag the whole thing to the doorway and across the road to where Yugi stands. When I get close enough, I take off my gun and put it down. I drop onto my belly and push the board beside me over the slippery gravel, trying to use the small pile of rubble on it as some kind of cover.

"What are you doing? Get away from me!" Yugi is virtually crying now. "I'm not kidding, Buffy. Next time he's going to kill you . . ."

"I'm not leaving. Just hear me out. I've got an idea."

"I don't mind dying," Yugi says in a barely audible whisper. "I just don't want to be a cripple and I don't want to take you with me."

"You won't, all right? So shut up, because none of this is helping." Sweat is dribbling from my forehead and into my eyes now. I wipe it away with the back of my filthy sleeve, smearing my forehead with mud. "I've got a tray of rubble. I'm going to push it until it touches the back of your boot. Right?"

"And?"

"And on the count of three you're going to run like hell and I'm going to shove it where your foot is."

To my surprise, Yugi just laughs. His laughter is manic and out of control. Tears stream down his face and his whole body shudders and jerks.

"For God's sake!" I shout, watching his trouser leg ripple. "Calm down!"

Somehow he manages to do it. Then he sighs and takes a deep, long breath. "Buffy, that's the stupidest thing I've ever heard."

I try not to let the hurt sound in my voice. "It's all I've got."

"If you're expecting me to run off and leave you to take the blast, then you've got another thing coming."

"Well, duh . . . I'm not just going to lie here. I'm going to crouch like a sprinter and leg it the other way. Come on," I reason, "this way we both have an equal chance."

What I don't tell him is that I'm unbuckling my body armor and wriggling out of it because it will slow me down. I'm not the world's greatest sprinter.

I can sense from the fall of Yugi's shoulders that he might be caving in, so I wait patiently before adding gently, "Yugi, we don't have all day."

"OK, OK. Are we going on three, or after three?"

"On three."

I brace myself and am just about to ask him if he is ready, when I feel the hairs on the back of my neck tingle. For some reason I have to look over my shoulder and there, on the side of the road, a flash of movement catches my eye. A wind has come from nowhere and raised a swirling dust eddy. From the midst of it a young Afghan girl emerges. She is about fourteen years of age, exquisitely pretty with piercing pale green eyes, and she is wearing a sun-bleached blue dress embroidered with flowers. Her black, tangled hair lifts in strands and wraps around her face as she walks, but she raises a delicate, pale hand and pulls it away from her lips. I didn't even notice her approach. She could be a suicide bomber or anything. And my gun is lying on the ground between us. She stops just a few feet away from it and watches me without speaking.

I don't believe it. I scream into the back of my arm until my throat is raw.

It's Yugi's panic that pulls me out of it. "Buffy, what is it? What's wrong?"

"Civilian," I croak. "Like this isn't hard enough."

"Get them away!"

Time is running out. The sniper could start taking potshots again anytime.

I yell at the girl, "GO! MOVE!" and wave my free arm at her, but she just gazes at me with those green eyes.

"Nielson! Where's the rest of your team?"

As if I didn't have enough problems Heidi chooses this moment to arrive in support. She drops behind the cover of the wall where Gizmo and I had been. Even at this distance I can tell she is furious with me.

I shout back, "Don't come any closer! Gizmo and Chip have gone to sort the sniper out."

Heidi's expression of fury is now mixed with irritation. "You shouldn't be on your own!"

Then I see her look beyond me at my discarded gun and then she clocks the girl. Her hard expression drops and all the color drains from her face.

The girl doesn't bat an eyelid, doesn't even seem to register Heidi's presence. She just stands there like a statue, watching me.

I look at Heidi. She's my superior. It's up to her to deal with this. But she looks stunned — no, more than that — she looks almost . . . frightened, her gun hanging uselessly at her side. It leaves me no choice. With my heart pounding in my ears I unclip my pistol and scream at the Afghan girl, "GO AWAY . . . *NOW*!" And then I let off three shots above my head.

"What are you doing? You're going to blow it!" Yugi is rattled. Both his legs are shaking uncontrollably now.

The girl still doesn't move. She looks almost puzzled.

Is she connected to the sniper? Carrying another bomb? At my briefing they told me that the Taliban use kids just like her, especially young girls.

I shout, "Corporal, what should I do?"

She looks like she might answer, but instead she falls back against the wall and shakes her head. I take it to mean she just wants me to deal with it, and I look back at the girl. Should I aim to kill her? Adrenaline courses like ice through my chest at the thought. Maybe I should, but I know I can't do it. Then a mixture of relief and fear floods through me as she pulls a faded red scarf up over her head, turns without a word, and walks slowly back toward the village. It seems an eternity before her slender figure shudders and evaporates into the heat haze.

I rest my head on my arms and try to block it all out, to refocus on what I'm about to do. Raw panic grips me, threatening to overwhelm me.

"Buffy . . ."

It is Yugi. His voice brings me back to this world. With an immense effort I force myself to open my eyes, to look at the back of his scuffed, dusty, trembling boot.

"Are you OK? It's just, I can't hold this much longer."

I'm not sure . . . I'm trying not to shake, but I can't help thinking about what might happen in the next few seconds. I don't want it to end here.

"Yes," I lie, but my voice betrays me, "and the next time you call me Buffy, I'm going to blow this thing myself. Are you ready?"

"Sorry, mate. Yes, yes, I'm ready now."

I take a deep breath, get to my haunches, and prepare to shove my panel of rubble. Just as I am about to start the countdown, bullets ricochet once more off the floor around us. They're coming in from virtually straight ahead of us.

"Duck!" I yell.

I can hear answering fire from Gizmo and Chip.

"I'm just going to do it. Get ready!"

Now the incoming fire doesn't stop. Hot, whipping shards of metal bounce around us. The sniper can see what I am about to do, and he's more desperate now. At any minute he is going to hit either me, Yugi, or the IED.

"ONE! TWO! *THREE!*"

On the last count, I shove my payload and run like all the demons of hell are at my back.

I have taken just six frantic, pounding paces when there is a rushing explosion behind me and a thud like someone has thrown a sack of rocks at my back. The impact hurls me toward the wall, and I hit the ground, rolling as a shower of hardened mud and debris falls all around me. My ears pop and in the eerie, whining silence that follows the blast, Chip's calm voice crackles over my headset. It is muffled and breathless — I can barely hear it.

"We got the sniper. Gizmo! Can you see Buffy and Yugi?"

Heidi's reply cuts across Gizmo's response. Her voice is hoarse. "Both down. Can't see much yet."

As the gray dust cloud falls slowly back to earth and the buildings opposite draw into focus through the fog, I'm just able to make out a huge crater. I feel like I've probably swallowed half of it. My mouth is dry and I'm having to spit mud.

Yugi's helmet is near me, still rocking slightly. And I can just make out a figure, covered in gray rubble, lying on the other side of the crater. It's not moving.

4

ALREADY I'M THINKING ABOUT YUGI AND WHAT I'm going to need from my medical kit if he's lost a limb, or worse . . . I try to calm my beating heart. The dust clears some more. I struggle up, desperate to do something, but I feel an arm grab mine to stop me. It's Heidi. Greg is running toward us from the cover of the wall.

Heidi shakes the blast debris off her helmet and mutters, "Cover me," to Greg as he arrives.

But before she has a chance to make a move the figure stirs and Yugi staggers to his feet, showering dust and rubble. He shakes his gray, matted hair and pokes at his ears with his finger. Even from here I can see that he's grinning. I feel like whooping and have to stop myself. It's my first day and already I've helped to save someone! When he catches sight of me, Yugi sticks up a thumb and jogs drunkenly toward the wall, picking his helmet up on the way. His cheesy smile is the best sight I've ever seen in my life.

Chip's voice crackles again. "Will somebody *please* tell me — are they OK?"

Heidi speaks into her mouthpiece as if nothing important has happened. "They're fine, Chip — stupid, but fine." Then she throws me a look filled with utter contempt.

After a whispered conversation with Chip and Gizmo, Heidi calls in coordinates for the casualties. There are two, apparently — Chip's and the one Heidi's team shot back in the town. I offer to help deal with the bodies, but Heidi almost snaps my head off. She leaves me waiting with the others until the medevac helicopters have left with thudding rotor blades and clouds of dust. Then we start the long walk back to the base. Heidi makes me wear the charred remains of my body armor all the way.

"You can replace that out of your wages," she tells me angrily, "and don't *ever* — and I mean EVER — leave your gun unattended again."

I can deal with the dressing-down. She's right, leaving my gun unattended was stupid, but I'm still on a high. Yugi is alive. My vest is still warm and filthy from the blast and I have to tie it together at one shoulder, but I don't feel the weight of it or the rest of my gear anymore. I'm going to keep it forever — like a memento of what I've achieved. Yugi insists on walking ahead of me like some guard of honor. He looks twitchy, like he might let off a few rounds at the slightest noise, if he feels it might be a threat to me.

Chip and Gizmo were relieved to see Yugi in one piece, but the reunion was strangely low-key. Neither will talk about the sniper. I guess you don't kill another human being and walk away unaffected. They both look grim, but it's a shock to see Chip subdued and not treating anything like a joke. It makes me feel uneasy. If you ask me, the more extroverted you are, the more you internalize the bad stuff. In training they said guys like Chip go home and get hit by post-traumatic stress. I decide I'll try to get both of them talking when we're back at base. Always the medic.

We have not marched far before a pounding headache begins to throb behind my eyes and soon I feel like my legs are going to give out. I'm physically and mentally exhausted, and this is just my first day. How the hell am I going to last the week?

I can feel Heidi's eyes boring into my back. What exactly is her problem? That I tried to save Yugi's life? Surely that can't be it. And it can't be jealousy over looks, either. By the way some of the guys look at her I can tell that they struggle with the concept that a woman can be so beautiful and so tough at the same time. Whereas my mum would probably burst into tears if she could see *me* now — no makeup, caterpillar eyebrows, and my short hair matted with dust. I look like one of the lads. To be fair I think I smell just as bad, too. Day one is almost over, I'm still alive and despite my exhaustion I'm beginning to think I might just make a real soldier.

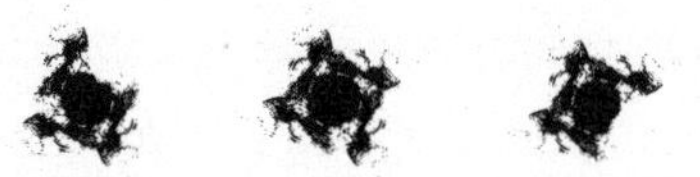

The minute we get back to base I go to get cleaned up. This time when I get to the shower, I make sure that I have eyeballed the surrounding rooftops before removing my towel, and even then I crouch as low as I can to wash. As the water cascades over me I feel like I'm in heaven. It tastes salty when it dissolves the dried-on sweat around my lips. It's like all the aches and fears of the day are running away in the scummy foam that forms in the mud under the plastic grating. But one memory clings to me stubbornly. Whenever I close my eyes all I can see is that girl, standing there, staring at me. My head feels like mush. She seemed to come out of nowhere, and that worries me. I wonder if I'm becoming superstitious. According to some of the guys back in Germany, that can happen out here.

An hour later and I'm getting myself hot and sweaty again looking for Yugi and Gizmo. The day is beginning to cool but the heat lingers — radiating out of the ground and the walls. I walk past the corner of the ammo store and find the guys sitting on sandbags in the shade cast by one of the outer walls. There are a couple of pomegranate trees visible just above it and a faint fruity smell wafts over on the breeze. This close to the base I'll bet the fruit is never picked and just lies out there where it falls, festering in the heat. Strangely it's not unpleasant and seems to keep the flies away from this side of the wall. It's obviously a good place to think. Yugi jumps to his feet like he's going to hug me, but Gizmo just stays where he is, his eyes closed and his head resting against the wall. He looks up as I drop beside him, shielding his eyes with a huge hand.

I smile at them, thinking how different this picture could have been without Yugi. "Nice little place you've got here. Where's Chip?"

"In the gym," Gizmo says, closing his eyes again.

I found the gym an hour ago, but Chip wasn't there. It's an area behind the armory, with some improvised weightlifting gear — basically a bunch of rocks in sacks suspended from the walls on rusty pulleys. There are even a few sandbags tied together to make a heavyweight punching bag. I picture Chip taking angry swings at it until he passes out from exhaustion.

"Can I get you something, Buffy?" Yugi rattles a bucket. It is filled with water, with a couple of cans of Coke and a bottle of spring water floating in it.

"No, thanks."

"Sure? I've been chilling it for an hour."

"Positive."

"Take one for later, then."

I smile and hold up my hand. "Really, I'm fine, Yugi."

Something is definitely up with Gizmo. Maybe the form here is not to talk about the bad stuff, but I'm new. Besides, I like tackling things head-on.

I ask him, "What happened with the sniper?"

Gizmo opens his eyes. I'm shocked to see that they're filling up. Now I feel bad for asking. So much for tackling things head-on.

"I'm sorry. We don't need to know."

"Best leave well alone, mate," Yugi agrees, with a sheepish shrug. "All I know is that I owe you guys — all of you."

With a deep breath, Gizmo pulls himself together and seems to make a decision. "The sniper — he was just a kid," he says finally. "Couldn't have been more than about twelve. We didn't know until we got to where he was hiding. By then he was dead already."

Now Yugi and I look at each other. Neither of us knows what to say. *A twelve-year-old kid? That's terrible.* For a moment I think of my brother, Jake. He's just one year older — thirteen. Then I remember the girl. It could have been a friend of hers.

I try to find some words, any words. "You couldn't have known. Nobody could. How could any of us have realized that it was a kid taking potshots?"

But I wonder: *Could we have done anything differently?*

Gizmo shakes his head. "It was a bit more than target practice, Buff . . . Ellie. That whole thing was a trap. Somehow he'd managed to get hold of an IED and lay it. Turned out to be an antipersonnel mine on top of a couple of antitank mines. You don't just pick those things up — not even round here. And another thing . . ."

"What?"

"He didn't run."

"What do you mean?"

"When he knew we were after him, any normal kid would have run like hell — either that or surrendered."

"You think he was fighting to the death?"

"You got that right. If I didn't know better, I'd say he wanted to die. I've seen enough of it out here. They're mad, all of these maniacs. Martyrdom is better than defeat."

"They're not all mad. And you know it."

Gizmo shrugs.

"And, as Buffy said, you couldn't have realized you were dealing with a kid," Yugi adds.

"Oh yeah? Well, that's where you're wrong. Ask Chip. We both should have known."

"Why?"

"Because an adult sniper would have just shot Yugi. Only a kid would have wasted time trying to blow up the IED."

He's right. I can't believe none of us thought about it. We were all too busy dealing with the situation to think clearly.

Yugi feels the need to fill the strained silence. "But you'll get over it, Gizmo. An insurgent is an insurgent, right?"

Gizmo pulls himself upright and claps a heavy hand between my shoulder blades. "Anyway, you were fantastic today."

I can't blame him for wanting a change of subject, but my mind is still on the kid. "If you say so."

Yugi agrees, pulling the ring on a dripping can of Coke and placing the soda in my hand — even though I'd said I didn't want one. "Yes, you were — I owe you . . ."

I don't want Yugi to feel that he owes me anything. He would do the same for me — we all know that. Anyway, after what Gizmo has told us, the thrill of saving Yugi's life is tarnished for me now. I give him back the can. "Don't be daft."

"No, really . . . I mean it."

"Please don't do this all night, Yugi," I say. "It's fine. You didn't want me to risk my neck anyway, so we're quits."

"What you did was crazy though." Gizmo smiles. "I'll bet you get some kind of medal."

Just then Jug appears round the corner of the building and strides up to us. With one rippling arm he pulls me into a vicelike hug and with the other he punches Gizmo's bicep. "Wassup, Gizmo, Yugi, *Buffy* . . ."

I was right — my nickname's gone viral. But for a moment even this interruption is a relief, until Jug spins me round to face him.

"I've been looking everywhere for you. The OC wants to see you — *now.*" He grins.

Yugi punches the air. "Yes! You're a hero, Buffy. Next thing you know the BBC will be out here."

"And he wants to see you, too, mate," Jug adds, watching the smile on Yugi's face freeze.

5

YUGI FILLS ME IN AS WE MAKE OUR WAY TO THE captain's office. "The OC's name is Steve McQueen. He's one of the oldest guys on the base . . ."

"What does that have to do with anything, Yugi?"

"Nothing." He hesitates. "But most of the squaddies think he's . . . well, you'll see. His name is a joke, too."

One which would have gone right over my head if my nan wasn't obsessed with that sixties actor. She's got all his films on DVD. All I can remember is shaggy-dog blue eyes, blond hair, and one of two looks: worried or an over-the-top intense frown. He was good-looking, though, if you're a nan.

We pass through a corridor of sandbags and enter what must have been part of an old Afghan farmhouse. It's got a thick, flat roof with a row of weathered beams jutting out all along the front. I feel as though there should be a nativity scene inside. Instead, the space has been divided up into separate rooms with more sandbags and tarps. I'm guessing from Yugi's look in that direction that the captain's office is at the back where the low evening light filters in shafts through gaps in the sandbag wall. I can hear two voices. One is Heidi's.

I should have seen it coming, really. Whenever I can, I try to see the good in people, and it always comes as a shock to me when someone I've done nothing to dumps on me. I am new here, but I suppose I would have found out sooner or later that Heidi is just the kind of person who can do this kind of thing. She is already at it when we get to McQueen's office. There is no door, just a thick tarp nailed to a makeshift wooden lintel wedged between the sandbags above our heads. We can hear every word.

McQueen sounds irritable. "I don't understand what you expect me to do about it, Corporal. We need another medic. Nielson is a medic. If she's not up to scratch, then it's your job to see she is."

"Then back me up on this, sir. That's all I ask. A little discipline will help me do *my job*."

"I don't know. I'm not sure I agree . . ."

"Nielson needs a firm hand."

I'm shocked. What have I done to her?

Yugi's surprised, too. He looks at me and mouths, "*What?*"

McQueen sounds exasperated, like she's been at him for hours and he's had enough. "On her first day?"

"*Especially* on her first day."

There's a heavy sigh from the captain. He can't be bothered to argue. "If you insist."

"I do, sir. Now, about the Americans . . ."

"Again, I don't know how many different ways I can tell you, Corporal. We are on the front line. Our choices are limited."

I can almost hear Heidi's teeth grinding. "There are plenty of other bases the Americans could use."

"And we're closest to the mountains. You of all people should know that this is a tactical decision. You're just going to have to grin and bear it. You won't have anything to do with them anyway. They'll only be here for a few days, if that."

So we are having American guests. Should be interesting. But why doesn't Heidi want them here?

Yugi grins at me and whispers, "Hot news! Chip's going to love this." He knocks on the doorpost.

"Enter!"

It turns out that the only thing the captain has in common with that old film star is blond hair and ears that stick out a little too far for comfort. He is seated behind a battered old desk, his face is drawn and prematurely lined, and Heidi is standing at his side. Her tanned face flushes as we enter. Anger at the interruption? I give her the dirtiest look I can manage. Then I realize it must be guilt for dumping on me. She's probably wondering how much we overheard. Good. Sit and spin.

"Ah, Private Wainwright," the captain says to Yugi. "Could have been a nasty outcome for you today. Glad you made it back."

He doesn't look glad. Worry lines dent his forehead like something is eating him, and he fiddles with a silver lighter which rests on the corner of his desk, spinning it like a top and stopping it with his index finger. When he realizes it's a distraction, he picks it up and puts it in his shirt pocket.

"Thank you, sir," Yugi replies, adding eagerly, "I wouldn't have if it hadn't been for —"

Still smarting, Heidi stamps her authority on the proceedings. "Zip it, Private."

McQueen's pale eyes rest on me, then he consults his notes and rubs his stubbled chin. "You must be Nielson."

"Sir."

Now that all the niceties are out of the way, his mouth opens and closes a few times as if he's not sure what to say. There is a long, long silence. So long it's embarrassing. I don't know where to put myself. So I focus on Heidi's scowling face, in the hope that she'll realize that she doesn't intimidate me, but I'm distracted by what's on the desk. Next to the captain's notepad is an open file. I recognize the crest on the top sheet. It belongs to the US Navy SEALs — elite troops, the equivalent of our Special Air Service. Not just any old Americans, then. I wonder what their mission is. It'll be important if a Sea, Air, and Land team is involved.

Finally the captain breaks the silence. "What you did was very brave, of course," he begins awkwardly, with an almost defiant glance at Heidi.

I'm embarrassed — what a doormat.

"And I do commend you for it, Private."

"Thank you, sir." I wait for the *but*. After Heidi's briefing, I can tell I'm not going to come out of this well.

"But . . . I can't have troops just taking things into their own hands, endangering themselves and the rest of the platoon."

That's so unfair! I forget myself. "What?" McQueen raises his eyebrows so I add, "Sir. With respect, how did I endanger the platoon?"

Heidi can't contain herself any longer. "You put the whole team at risk with your heroics! You left your weapon by the side of the road for anyone to pick up! And Chip and Gizmo should have known better. Believe me, the captain's going to have words with them, too, when Chip has had time to get over . . ."

She checks herself but Yugi and I both know she's talking about the kid.

"You should all have taken cover and requested support, Nielson. Pinned the shooter down until help arrived. We have disposal experts. How could any of you have known that there was only one IED?"

"We didn't. We just acted to save Yugi's life," I say angrily. "What was I supposed to do? Sit and watch him blow himself up? We did request support, but your team was already engaged."

"Yes, we were engaged," Heidi says through gritted teeth, "and if things had gone badly, which they very nearly did, you would have been totally isolated."

"Seriously, sir," Yugi adds in my defense, "that thing could have gone up at any second."

"Yes, well" — McQueen holds up his hand — "that's as may be. The corporal — and *I*," he qualifies hastily, "believe that Nielson acted rashly, and although there was a good outcome on this occasion, she did endanger herself and others."

Heidi smiles at me.

I'm not going to give her the satisfaction, so I keep my face still and hope my cheeks don't color up.

The captain pauses. "And then there is the rather more serious matter . . ."

"Sir?"

"Of shooting live rounds at a civilian child."

I almost choke. Why the hell would Heidi tell him I'd shot *at* the girl? She was there; she saw what I did.

I say quietly and firmly, "I didn't shoot *at* her." I really want to add, *"and at least I wasn't peeing in my boots,"* but I hold my tongue.

"Sir, I can vouch for —" Yugi begins.

Heidi does not give him chance. "Vouch for what, Yugi? Your back was to her the whole time."

McQueen straightens up in his chair and sighs deeply. Looks like he's had enough. His eyes flick between us and — just fantastic — they settle on me. I brace myself for the lecture. "As you know, we are here both to push back the insurgents and to gain the trust and support of the indigenous people. My role" — he's sounding really pompous now — "is to bring together the coalition, the Afghan police, and local tribal leaders. It's not our place to question it — even the interior minister Zalmai Khan thinks it's madness — but President Karzai wants to start talks with the Taliban before Western forces leave the country. For good or ill that process starts *here*" — he thumps the table — "on the ground."

"But, sir," I say, ignoring the politics and bringing him back to the girl, "she was in danger and wouldn't move! I let off a couple of rounds above my head. We were being shot at, and Yugi here was standing on an IED that could have taken both of us and the civilian girl at any second. I didn't have time to reason with her."

"Even so, I can't have troops jeopardizing the fragile trust we are trying to build. Your actions were brave, nobody's doubting that," McQueen says firmly as Heidi shifts slightly, "but they were also foolish, and it is with some regret that I have to put you on a warning."

Yugi looks like he is about to burst, but when he reads my glance, he clams up.

I grit my teeth. "Yes, sir."

Heidi says quietly, "By the way, Nielson. Do you want to know *who* we engaged while you were playing the hero?"

How would I know? Insurgents, Taliban — who else? "I don't know what you mean."

"It was another group of kids — and they very nearly got the better of us. We killed one of them before we knew what was happening. The youngest yet — a boy of about ten — just in case you're interested."

"What?" I'm shocked. Another boy? Heidi just stands there, watching her words sink in. "Do you think they were Taliban?"

McQueen answers for her. "We don't know. This may be an isolated incident. Maybe these kids just found a couple of guns and were playing at soldiers. God knows they see enough of it. Whatever the truth of the matter, the net result is that we have killed two civilian children and threatened a third. I don't think I need to tell you how serious this is."

There is a tense silence in which the captain looks at me long and hard, like he is trying to decide if I am going to be trouble. Then he falls back in his chair and turns to Heidi. "Corporal Larson."

"Sir?"

"We need to find out why we've suddenly got minors shooting at us and possibly laying IEDs. I want you to get into the local community tomorrow with Hammed and your team and see what you can find out. Do anything you can to smooth things over. I'm going to have the tribal elders call a *jirga* and meet me here as soon as they can. With any luck we'll have some answers before these Americans arrive. Because you can be sure they'll be full of questions."

He closes the SEAL file on his desk. As I watch him shift in his chair to look at me again, I suddenly feel for him. His job must be a massive nightmare. Apart from the fact that he's responsible for so many lives, he has to keep everyone happy — his superiors, friendly Afghans — us. And the last thing he wants is for the Americans to think he's losing control.

I so want to tell him that "winning hearts and minds" is one of the reasons I joined the army, that I'm for real, but if I say anything now it's just going to look like an excuse.

Heidi hardly says a word when we bunk down for the night, and I wrestle with whether or not I should confront her about how she bad-mouthed me to McQueen. I'm new and I don't want to rock the boat, but she was unfair and she knows it. Confronting Heidi could go either way though. It's a gamble. In the end, as her breathing is starting to get heavier, I decide that I have to take the chance.

I whisper into the creaking silence, half hoping that she is asleep, "You can say what you like about me to the brass, Corporal, but both you and I know that I didn't shoot *at* that girl. And *I know* you were scared of her for some reason. So I don't care how bad it gets — I'm going to do my job so well that no one will be able to pick holes in it. And do you know what else? I'm going to find out who that girl is."

Heidi doesn't answer, but I know she's heard me.

6

HAMMED IS A TALL AFGHAN POLICE OFFICER. HE comes striding through the gates like he is on a mission while we are waiting in the compound to set out on my second patrol. Chip and Gizmo have already told me a bit about him but I like to form my own opinions. Beneath a grubby, flat *Pakol* hat and a tangle of graying beard his face is scored with deep lines and he has a haunted expression. I guess working for the coalition means he will have a price on his head, so it's no wonder he looks preoccupied. When we pull out of the country, he'll be on his own. The guy's got guts. I'm here with unbelievable backup, but he just has a small group of officers and his principles. I know hardly anything about him but already I admire him. Even to think about working with the coalition in Helmand has got to be dangerous. If you ask me, Hammed is the kind of person who wants to change things for the better and is prepared to die trying.

Chip is back to normal, apart from the dark circles under his eyes and two grazed, swollen fingers on his right hand, which he has strapped together with tape and an old popsicle stick. Fortunately his trigger finger is still intact. He nudges my arm. "I hear Captain Spineless decided to pass on the gallantry medal, then."

I laugh. "I didn't want it anyway. You OK?"

"Why wouldn't I be?" he mutters.

My cue to draw him out. Get him talking about things for once. "I heard about the boy."

Chip looks up and blood flushes his cheeks. "Gizmo? Bloody hell!" He looks around. "Where is he?"

"Go easy on him. He needed to talk about it — that's a good thing." I nod to his injured hand. "Maybe you should try it sometime. Anyway, you can't expect to keep something like that quiet. Not here. It's important news. One of the reasons they wanted to talk to me yesterday."

Now Chip's looking like he's mad at me. "Oh? Why the hell are they talking to *you* about my kill?"

"Because the other casualty was a child, too. McQueen wants us to find out why kids are trying to kill us."

Chip looks away for a moment, unable to speak. He watches

Heidi greet Hammed and it's a while before his shoulders drop and he can look at me again. He says gruffly, "That'll be why Hammed's coming, then. His English is rough, but he is the best in the area. McQueen's always using him as an interpreter on so-called 'friendship' missions and at his pointless *jirgas*."

"And a *jirga* is . . . ?"

"It's when the tribal elders come together to talk about stuff."

"Then they're not pointless. They're building trust."

"Whatever. The buggers are still shooting at us, aren't they? Another year and he'll be able to do it himself anyway. The tosser's been learning Pashto."

If Chip thinks that will make me think less of the captain, he's wrong. I'm impressed. At least the guy is trying. I watch as McQueen joins the corporal. Hammed looks agitated but Heidi hasn't spoken to him yet beyond that initial greeting. Must have been waiting for the captain. At my "cultural orientation" — a fifteen-minute documentary with a Q&A session — I was told that most Afghan men are very awkward around women. In conversation, they told us, an Afghan man will answer you while looking at one of the guys. I know it shouldn't, but that really pisses me off.

McQueen says, "*Salaam*, Hammed. Thank you for coming."

They shake hands awkwardly.

Then the captain mumbles something that I miss. Sounds apologetic.

"Is not good. Why you killing the children?" Hammed demands angrily. To my surprise he's engaging Heidi eyeball to eyeball, and I wonder if my briefing was right.

Heidi is touchy. "We weren't aware they were children," she snaps.

The captain holds up his hand. "Did you know either of them, Hammed?"

There's a pause while he takes a deep breath. "Maybe, yes." Judging by the haggard look on his face, I wonder if Hammed must have come here after being asked to identify the bodies.

Heidi's face softens. "Where do you think they come from?"

"Maybe mountain village." Hammed sounds a bit cagey to me, like he doesn't want to go into it. "They wild places."

"So what were they doing down here?" Heidi presses.

Hammed shrugs.

I can't help myself. "Permission to speak, sir?"

The captain looks exasperated but he nods, and I find myself actually walking over to join them. It's something I have to do, despite the nerves. The image of the girl won't leave me — the blue dress, the green eyes. And I want the captain to see Heidi's reaction when I mention her. "Sir, I wondered about the girl . . . Do you think she was with them?"

"Of course not," Heidi says, but now that haunted look is back in her eyes. Why is she so freaked out by a young Afghan girl?

"Perhaps Hammed should be the judge," McQueen tells her.

"The girl? You kill girl, too? Aiy!" Hammed wails at McQueen.

"We didn't!" I say. "She was just there. Very pretty — black hair, light green eyes. About fourteen years old and wearing a blue dress embroidered with flowers."

For the briefest of moments, Hammed's eyes meet mine. He seems relieved.

Heidi is chewing at her bottom lip, really agitated. I could swear she's holding back tears. "The girl is irrelevant, OK? So just drop it."

I am stunned. Heidi knew the civilian girl. She definitely did. I remember the fear on her face, the way her gun hung uselessly at her side.

"With respect, how can you say that?"

"You're not a part of this conversation, Private," Heidi returns, "so butt out."

McQueen backs her up. "Thank you, Private."

"Sir." I look at Heidi, but she avoids my eyes. Every time I think about what happened yesterday I can see the girl vividly, as clear as if she's standing right next to me, and I know that she wasn't there by accident. I wish I could get her out of my head. It's clear I'm not going to get any answers, I'm just a private, so I make my way back to the guys. They're all waiting patiently, sitting on their backpacks. Chip's fiddling with a grenade that's clipped to his body armor.

"What was all that about?" Yugi asks.

"The girl at the IED yesterday, I think she was involved with the sniper."

"And Heidi doesn't?" says Chip.

"Keep your voice down!"

Yugi mutters dreamily, "It's the strangest thing . . . she was behind me, and I couldn't turn round to see her, but I keep getting these flashbacks, and every time I do I swear I see her as clearly as I see you guys."

"It was a traumatic event," I tell him.

"Yeah, but this is so vivid. I mean, what color was her dress?"

"You tell me, if it's so clear."

"Blue . . . a very faded sky blue, and there were flowers on it."

"How the hell . . . ?"

"What?" Chip and Gizmo are looking between us, not understanding.

"He's right — about everything."

Gizmo snorts. "A lucky guess."

"Yeah, but the flowers? How would he have known about the flowers? I mean . . ."

"What else is a girl's dress going to have on it?" Chip laughs. "Gizmo's right — it's a lucky guess. Anyway, Yugi wouldn't know a girl's dress from his own arse."

"Oi!" Yugi protests.

"What?" says Chip. "You've never been closer than a mile to a girl wearing anything other than cammies, and the only time you've ever seen one out of them was Buffy — and she hardly counts."

I punch his arm, hard. And I know there's no way that was just a lucky guess. There is something weird about that girl. In fact, it's beyond weird.

As we pick up our kit and make our way to the gates the rumble of several heavy diesel engines is carried to us on the wind. Phil, a lanky gunner, clambers onto the roof of one of the crappers and shields his eyes with his hand. I don't know how he can stand the smell up there.

Heidi calls, "What's going on, Phil?"

"Three Hummers," he tells her, relaxing back onto his backside and letting his legs dangle over the side. "Looks like Uncle Sam's arrived."

"Fantastic," Chip says, his face lighting up. "Decent poker players. I've had enough of you losers — you're too easy."

For some reason Gizmo looks over at Heidi and asks her, "You all right?"

She's looking at the dust cloud, lost in thought. At the sound of his voice she pulls herself out of it. "I'm fine," she says through gritted teeth. "Why the hell wouldn't I be?"

Yugi asks, "Why do you think they're here?"

I pitch in. "I'll bet you anything it's related to those kids."

"A betting girl, eh?" Chip's mind is stuck in a rut. "How'd you like to learn —"

"No, thanks." I'm not interested, especially now that Heidi is docking my pay.

The gates open and Heidi gives us the command to start moving. We file out of the base and onto the road while the Hummers fly past us close enough to touch. The *beep beep* of the horns is comical for such a huge vehicle, sounds really out of place, and a couple of the Americans lift their hands as if to add weight to the greeting. I can't resist the urge to peer inside as the Hummers pass me. It looks like there are five men in each vehicle, two in the front and three in the back. In the passenger seat of the first one I glimpse a guy in a khaki baseball cap and shades. A baseball cap! I've heard Special Forces like to travel light, but it seems really overconfident to me. The guy's bronzed arm rests on the frame of the open window and a sharp-looking tribal tattoo is just visible below the sleeve of his T-shirt.

I notice Heidi shoot a look in the same direction. It's the first time I've seen any real emotion in her face. She looks tired, almost hopeless, and her shoulders sag. Turning her back on the Hummers, she quickens her pace, gesturing to us all to follow, while the American vehicles spread out and jerk to a halt in the compound.

A flustered McQueen runs out of one of the crappers in a cloud of cigarette smoke, tugging frantically at his fly.

"Gives a whole new meaning to the 'special relationship,' don't you think?" Jug says loudly.

There's a scattering of appreciative laughs.

Chip adds, "He's just pleased to see them . . ." to more.

The way the captain is pulling at his zipper, it looks like it may be stuck. He gives up, stamps the stub of his cigarette out, and waits for the Hummer door to open. To my dismay, that's all I get to see before we move out. All too soon I've left the safety of the base, with Chip beside me, scanning for mines and, as memories of yesterday tug at me, I find myself hoping I make it back here to meet them.

7

EVERYONE IS EDGY WHEN WE LEAVE THE DIRT ROAD, much farther up than yesterday, and make our way to the north bank of Helmand River. Today we're heading off-road and onto the plains. It's a more heavily populated area. Apparently Hammed thinks people in the villages out here may have been feeding the kids from the mountains and will know more about them than anyone. We're going to start at a village called Khuaja and then go on to another, Darzab.

Today's route takes us through a lowland landscape with dry tracks, sunbaked walls, and derelict houses that look like the relics of the eighties war with Russia. Either side of the dirt tracks it's still green though. And even I can tell that this is prime ambush territory. There is plenty of dense cover and irrigation ditches edged with tall, flat grasses that make perfect trenches.

We make our way through lush fields of maize, heady marijuana, and poppies. Opium poppies, I realize. Afghanistan is the world's biggest producer of opium. And it makes big money. That's one reason the Taliban are fighting to the death to protect it. If we're stupid enough to buy it they'll use the money to fund their war, thank you very much. Walking through field after field of the stuff, I begin to wonder how many of the crops the Afghans grow are actually legal. The heat is oppressive again, and flies swarm around my face, attracted by the salty beads of sweat that glue my eyelids together when I blink. After a while it becomes too much effort to bat them away.

It looks like Chip has drawn the short straw today. He fills in some details for me without being asked. I'm touched that the guys are trying so hard to help me fit in. "The people here are tribal, suspicious of everyone and everything, especially us," he tells me. "No one wants to be seen talking to coalition troops because the Taliban are watching — believe me, the ragheads are always watching."

"Ragheads? Come on, Chip. Hammed could hear you."

"What? Relax, it's not racist. It's what they wear on their heads. And don't worry about him — he's heard it all before.

Anyway, Mother Teresa, what would you like me to call them? I can give you some alternatives . . ."

"I don't know. I just think if you respect your enemy, eventually they'll respect you."

Chip looks at me like I'm mad. "Bloody hell, Buffy! If the *insurgents* want me to pay them a compliment they can stop aiming bullets at my friggin' head. Now, as I was saying, they've got eyes everywhere and they have lots of places to hide." He pokes at a dense, waist-high bush as we pass it and points into the trees with his rifle. "So keep your eyes peeled for dangling legs."

I laugh until I realize he's serious.

We march on in silence, suffering under the weight of our gear, on the rough, uneven terrain that makes us trip and stumble, and in the unrelenting heat. I can see that Chip is right about the suspicion; even Hammed struggles to get passing locals to engage with him.

When we get to Khuaja, the inhabitants emerge from their shabby dwellings and lean in doorways to watch us with barely concealed hatred. A middle-aged man with a long, straggly beard and narrow, angry eyes steps out of the dark entrance of his house to look at us. From his air of authority it is clear that he has some say in the village. Loosely gripped in his left hand is an automatic rifle. He barks something at Hammed in Pashto. It is not hard to work out what he might be saying, but before Hammed can respond, Heidi raises her gun. Flanked by Jug and Greg, she takes a couple of steps forward.

"Drop it!" she shouts, indicating the rifle and then the floor with her SA80.

The guy doesn't even register her presence, just speaks again to Hammed. The rifle swings lightly in his grip.

It looks like things could turn nasty. Suddenly my hands feel way too slippery. I wipe my trigger hand dry and test my hold.

"What did he say?" Heidi asks Hammed.

"He say, 'This *my* village,' and he don't take orders from woman."

"We'll see about that." Heidi gives the nod to Greg, who strides forward to disarm the guy.

The Afghan bares his teeth and points his index finger at Heidi as if to shoot her. Then he places his gun at his feet and puts his hands in the air. Greg kicks the gun away and frisks him.

We waste a couple of hours going from house to house. Pretty much everywhere we go in the village it's the same story. Those who do talk say they know nothing about the children we had engaged, and everywhere else we are met with a wall of silence. But we do find evidence that people are leaving food for someone — two baskets half filled with pomegranates and dried fruit left at the side of the road.

It's another hour's trek to the next village in the searing heat. My legs ache like hell after yesterday and I'm getting what must be a soldier's worst nightmare — especially out here — a sodding blister. I have to stop to deal with it, cutting and placing a small moleskin doughnut over the bubble of skin and spraying on some liquid bandage, which hardens to form a hard, waterproof barrier. Thankfully it seems to work, at least for the moment, but I'll need to pop it when we get back to base. It's about mid-afternoon by the time we approach Darzab and walk around its crumbling defenses to find the way in. We have just rounded a corner when the unmistakable rattle of automatic gunfire sends us scrambling for cover in the irrigation ditch that runs along this side of the village.

Gizmo is the last in. Rounds whizz past him and whip chunks out of the village wall. He's swearing as he throws himself at us and virtually dives headfirst into the water. Chip and I have to grab his arms so his head doesn't go under. I'm small and he almost takes me with him, but I manage to hold on — just. He rewards me with a sheepish smile when we heave him upright against the suction of the water. "Thanks. That was a bit close for comfort."

Chip grunts. "I don't think they were actually aiming at you."

I'm breathless and soaked in churned-up muddy water. "How can you tell?"

He taps his ear. "Listen and learn, Buffy."

Chip's right. When I stop to listen, I can actually get a sense of the direction the firing is coming from by the whipping sound the rounds make. I can even see traces as they cut through the air. The gun battle is between fighters in the village and another group in dense cover in the fields a few hundred meters to our right. They are using different weapons as well. I recognize the loose rattle from the village — the same weapons that were used against us yesterday. They are answered by tighter, crisper rounds from the fields. I'd say the ones in the field sound a lot like ours.

For the moment, though, all we can do is watch. We can't engage because we have no idea who is friend and who is foe. For all we know we could be caught between two warring Taliban factions, in which case I hope we'll just let them fight it out. Heidi calls in to base to see if any other coalition or special forces are in the area, and while we wait for information the firefight seems to move away from our position and much nearer to the village.

Heidi scrambles closer to Yugi, batting flies away from her face. "Looks like some local feud."

"So what do we do?" Yugi asks.

"I want to know *exactly* what we are dealing with before we step in. You take Jug and see who's out in the fields. I want to know numbers and what they are carrying. Chip?"

I can tell Chip is just itching to do something. "Yeah?"

"Take Nielson and see what's going on in the village. Don't take any stupid risks, and radio me — same thing. I don't need you to go in. Just tell me what you see."

The way Heidi tells us not to take risks, I'm beginning to wonder if the comment is aimed at Chip, too. He is a bit too keen to get into action. Maybe Heidi was right that we should have stayed together yesterday. It was him who decided to go after the sniper, after all, splitting up the team.

Chip looks narked. "Nielson? Don't you think I should take someone more experienced?"

I'm thinking that now *he* has a problem with me, when Heidi says knowingly, "I think she's up for it."

She definitely heard what I said last night, then. Chip's just protecting me.

So I answer firmly, "And you're right."

I follow Chip as he runs at a crouch along the sun-bleached, crumbling wall of the village, and the sporadic *rat-a-tat* of gunfire grows louder as we near the corner. My breathing is ragged. My heart is pounding in my ears. It's like my helmet is amplifying my mortality, like it's afraid I'll forget that underneath all this protection I'm just flesh and blood.

"How're you liking the front line, Buffy?" Chip grunts as we run.

"I didn't realize I'd see quite so much action."

He grins at me over his shoulder. He's actually enjoying this. "Get used to it. It's normal."

Whoever has been attacking from the cover of the fields has begun to change position again. It seems that most of their fighters must have entered the town now. The looser-sounding gunfire is coming from the other side of the wall, in short staccato bursts, and it's sounding more desperate.

When he reaches the end of the wall, Chip falls to his haunches and waits for me drop beside him. He looks around the corner and then silently waves me past.

The wall continues in front of me for a few meters until it meets a rotting gatepost where a wide gap yawns. When I reach it, I crouch to peer around and into the village. Flakes of dry white paint come off the post as I steady myself against it, and they stick to the palm of my hand. Nearby, colorful strings of washing hang from the windows to dry, gathering dust in the sweltering heat. Some of it is ripped apart by incoming rounds, and scraps of material flutter to the floor. Straight ahead the main street squeezes its way through a clutter of flat-roofed buildings. Bullets are hammering chunks out of the mud walls.

I see a terrified woman pull the wooden shutters on her window closed, as if they will protect her, and then, to my horror, the girl in the blue dress. She steps calmly out of an alley into the middle of it all, as if nothing is happening. And once again she's looking right at me with those pale green eyes.

What is she doing here?

I can hear Chip talking on the radio, telling Heidi that the fight seems to have moved entirely into the village. I look back at the girl, willing her to move. She's going to get herself killed if she stays there. A bullet hits the wall near her head. The dust spray makes her blink involuntarily, and I get the feeling that she won't, or can't, move unless I go to her. There has to be something I can do, some way to make her get out of the way. I wave my arm wildly, trying desperately to make her understand that she has to move, but, just as she did yesterday, she stands her ground, like she doesn't care whether she lives or dies.

I am angry with her and afraid for her all at the same time. I wonder if she has some weird mental problem or a death wish. Maybe she's deaf and dumb? But she must see the impact of those bullets, surely. I mean, what does she think she's doing? In the end I can't watch it any longer. I get to my feet and yell at her, "GET OUT OF THE WAY, YOU STUPID CHILD!"

Chip shouts from behind me, "WHAT THE HELL ARE YOU PLAYING AT? GET DOWN!"

That's when the bullet hits.

8

THE GIRL'S PRETTY HEAD LURCHES SIDEWAYS, SPURTing blood from just below the chin, and the force of the bullet throws her like a rag doll back into the alley and out of my sight. It is so sudden and so violent, this contrast between innocence and the wild reality of war, that I think I might throw up. I've never seen anyone shot before, let alone a kid. I need the wall for support and, while I pull myself together, I can see that sickening, bloody impact every time I blink.

Pressing the radio button on my gun, I sprint into the village, making for the nearest cover. "Civilian down," I tell Chip breathlessly. "A girl. Get backup!"

Chip calls me all the names under the sun, but he still follows my lead, leveling his gun with one hand and radioing for help with the other, as we dash from cover to cover into the hostile, ramshackle place. The gunfire, always ahead of us, recedes once more. It seems to be coming from farther down the street and a little to our left. Then, with a sudden frenzy, it splutters and echoes to a halt.

An eerie silence falls when we near the spot where the girl was shot, broken only by the hiss of wind in the trees beyond the village walls and distant voices reverberating along the alley, anxious and clipped. Chip looks at me and I know he has heard them as well — children — then the patter of bare feet running away. Are they fighting here, too? The same group of kids? When we reach the corner of the alley, we find wet crimson blood trickling down the whitewashed wall, drying to a congealed brown crust even as we watch.

With a glance at Chip to see if he is ready to cover me, I get my SA80 ready and throw myself against the opposite wall, sweeping the shadows of the alley with it. I expect to find the injured girl sprawled at my feet, but she is nowhere to be seen.

When Chip joins me, he points silently at the floor.

There, a trail of dark, wet stains lurches along the alley and disappears from sight where the buildings, deep in shadow, bend in a lazy arc to our right.

I press on along the passage.

Chip hisses at me through the headset, his voice barely audible, "For God's sake, Buffy, slow down."

The girl has lost a lot of blood so I guess she does not have much time left. I need to find her quickly or the whole dangerous enterprise will be futile. I'm frustrated, but Chip is right. We have to be cautious. Just around the bend, shaded from the fierce sun by close-built walls, we come across an open doorway. A bloody handprint is smeared on the door frame like a calling card. Chip is unclipping a grenade, but he stops when I shake my head at him. For the second time in as many days I realize that the training just doesn't prepare you for the real thing.

We take up positions either side of the entrance and, after taking a deep breath, I give him a hand signal and we enter.

  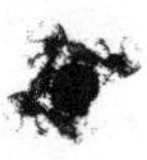

It is dark inside after the glare of the sunbaked walls. After yesterday I'm more prepared, and I will my pupils to widen, to probe the recesses of the room. Insurgents could be hiding anywhere and, in the light of the doorway, we are sitting targets.

To our relief we are greeted with nothing more than the creak and groan of old woodwork. Shafts of sunlight filter through dilapidated, bullet-riddled shutters and illuminate a sparse living area. A threadbare couch has been used as cover and it has been shot to pieces. Bits of stuffing and the splintered wooden frame lie scattered on the floor around it. Eerily, white puffs of cushion stuffing drift across the floor as we disturb the calm, still air. Just past the couch and to the left is a small kitchen with a single gas camping stove set on an old wooden box. The smell of cordite is heavy in the air. It burns our lungs.

At the far corner of the room to our right, a homemade ladder leans at an angle against the wall and disappears through a rough square hole to the floor above. The rungs are sticky with blood.

We look at each other.

There's no way I'm going to get through the gap with my backpack on so I slip it off and lean it against the wall. Silently, I make sure Chip understands that I am going to go first. This is my call. I should be the one to risk my neck. So I climb the ladder one-handed, with my gun at the ready. When I'm near the top, I hold my breath and my finger tightens around the trigger.

With a silent prayer I swallow my fear and launch myself up the last few rungs. My head and the barrel of my gun clear the opening simultaneously and, as my eyes pass floor level, I catch a flash of that faded blue dress. Thick, syrupy heat clings to me as I climb into the room. A thin voile curtain draped across the open window is in flames and the splintered shutters are beginning to scorch and blacken. The walls around it are pockmarked with bullet holes and splattered with blood. And the girl is there, wreathed in billowing smoke, crouching next to the twisted body of a young boy who seems to have been blown backward by the momentum of whatever has hit him. He is lying motionless in a dark, spreading pool.

The girl's back is to me and she makes no attempt to move. On the floor, a few centimeters from the boy's limp, half-closed hand, is a Kalashnikov assault rifle.

I scramble through the opening, whispering, "It's OK — I'm a friend." But I don't drop my guard and I keep my gun pointed at the girl the whole time.

She stands, getting to her feet and turning to face me in one fluid movement. When I see her features, I almost fall back on Chip, who is trying to follow me through the opening. The girl's eyes are bloodshot and wet with tears. Not only that, there is no blood on her neck or her dress. Not even a scratch. Just pure, smooth olive skin. She steps back from the injured boy, from me, framed by the fluttering, burning curtain, and watches me with those haunting green eyes while I look around the room.

I whisper, "Who are you?" But she does not answer me. "Are you real?" As soon as I say it I know I'm being stupid. Of course she's real — I could reach out and touch her if I want to. I'm not going to let this place affect me like it seems to have affected Heidi. I swear I'm not. My training kicks in. The boy on the floor is the casualty, the priority.

"Buffy, what's going on?" Chip asks me from the ladder. "I can't get through the opening and you're blocking my sight."

"The girl's here and there's a male casualty. It's another kid. I need my pack."

He disappears, and seconds later my pack is shoved up through the hole. At the same time the rattle of gunfire opens up again briefly. It sounds like it could be our guys coming into the town, but I can't be sure.

Chip's nervous about it, too. "I'm going to keep watch down here. Shout if you need me."

I hold up my hand so the girl can see I don't want to hurt her. "Friend . . ."

But all the time I'm wondering, is she mute or doesn't she understand English? And where the hell's her injury? My eyes are telling me there is another kid bleeding to death on the floor here, but my head is telling me it should be her. *She was shot — I saw it.*

Probing the girl's chin and neck one last time with my eyes, I tell her, "Step away from the gun," and point at the Kalashnikov with my rifle. My tone is harsh because I'm really shaken up now, feeling like my judgment is clouded, certain that the heat and stress are making me see things. Doubt grips my stomach and twists it into a knot, but I know I can't go there. I have to be able to trust my eyes, out here most of all. *Pull yourself together, Nielson.* What the hell is happening to me?

To my surprise and relief she seems to understand this time. She backs off. When she has reached the bloody, bullet-riddled wall by the window I kneel beside the boy and check his carotid artery for any sign of life. There is a faint, whispering pulse, but it's fading and when I tear open his filthy jacket, I have to stifle a gasp. His torso is full of bubbling crimson holes. I don't carry enough trauma dressings to deal with this number of entry wounds. There is nothing I can do for the kid but make him comfortable. He's dying.

As I bend over him and lift his head the boy's eyes open. He looks about sixteen. I have a sudden memory of my brother, Jake, his head bent over his guitar practicing chords.

"It's OK, I'm here to help you. What's your name, sweetie?" I ask.

He tries to turn his head and spit at me, but he doesn't have the strength. Instead, foamy saliva mingled with blood trickles from the corner of his mouth.

I look at the girl. Tears are falling from her eyes and rolling down her cheeks. I get it. She loves him.

With some of the wipes from my pack I gently stroke the blood from his forehead, wondering if he needs morphine. Doesn't look like it. A smile flickers across his young face. But it isn't for me. He's remembering something or seeing someone else now. An agony of grief washes over me as I watch, and I have to bury my feelings beneath a facade of professionalism. I've seen pictures in training, been told what to expect, but I've never seen anyone dying before. And I never thought that the first time would be a kid. My eyes sting and I squeeze them shut. *Focus, Nielson! Don't let yourself think about it.*

He coughs his name, "Farshad," and his eyes flicker, unseeing. "I bury her . . . in cave."

The kid knows some English, then. But he's hallucinating about something. I stroke his forehead and whisper, "It's all right, I'm here . . ." I turn to the girl. "Is he from here — the village?" She does not answer. "Taliban?"

Recognition lights up Farshad's eyes briefly. He focuses what's left of his strength, his breathing gurgling with blood, and answers for her, "Young Martyrs hate Taliban."

"Don't talk," I tell him while my mind spins with what he's just said. Young Martyrs? Does he mean the kids fighting us? And they're fighting the Taliban, too?

But he breathes, "Hate you, too. We kill all murderers."

I look at the girl, but she has turned her back to us. She is looking through the flaming voile curtain at the mountains.

Farshad's brown eyes are staring right at me now. They blink once and then he turns his face to the girl at the window. His wrinkled brow relaxes and a single word falls from his mouth, mingled with crimson saliva, "Aroush?"

I can't tell if it's a name, a word, or just his dying gasp, but in response the girl looks over her shoulder. Her mouth moves and her words tingle in my head like wind chimes. *"Salāmun alaykum . . ."* Then she bows her head and her long black hair cascades down and covers her face.

This final effort to speak proves too much for Farshad. When his face turns back toward mine, life leaves his shattered body with a wheezing sigh.

I reach down to close his eyelids and blackness engulfs me. I can't tell if it is grief, fatigue, or that all the oxygen is being burned up by the fire but I have to put my hand out to stop myself falling to the floor. At the same instant I feel a wind rushing through the oppressive room, and I find my vision clearing. I'm kneeling over the boy's body. His blood is still warm and liquid, soaking into my trousers, sticking them to my knees. What is happening to me? I shake my head to clear the black spots that still float before my eyes. When I raise my head to look at the window, my jaw drops.

In the background Chip's concerned voice is asking, "Buffy, are you all right? Buffy, answer me!"

But I can't. The girl has disappeared.

9

MY FIRST REACTION IS TOTALLY ILLOGICAL. I AM pissed off. I needed to talk to her. She's the reason Chip and I risked our necks. I wanted to know who she was, where she was from. My head is full of questions with no bloody answers. And the Young Martyrs? I look at Farshad's body. What a waste. Why? Why are they doing this?

When Chip's head pops up through the opening in the floor I realize she has to be with him.

"Buffy, thank God! Are you all right? There was a crash. And a load of rubble fell into the street."

"Did you catch her?"

Chip gawps like he can't process my words. They're simple enough, surely. "Did I catch who?"

I look at him. "The girl from the IED, she was here. She can't just have *gone*."

Chip points and I realize that the window frame is no longer there. All that remains is a ragged, smoke-blackened hole. "Look, the whole window's fallen out. Maybe she went with it. Really, Buffy, what's wrong with you? Are you telling me half the building blew out and you didn't notice a friggin' thing?"

I scramble to my feet and peer out of the opening and into the street below. Splinters of burning debris are scattered on the floor, but the girl is nowhere to be seen. I'm so sick of this place, even though I've only been here a couple of days. I want home so badly I can almost taste it. To go window-shopping with Mum. To smell fresh-ground coffee and laugh at Jake and my dad arguing over football results. The crumpled body of the boy, unloved and lonely in the corner of this dirty, blasted room, is breaking my heart. It makes me want to scream.

"Let's get out of here," I say, but my voice is dry and cracked.

Chip nods, but doesn't move. He's seen the boy's body. He's trying to calm his breathing, and his eyes are wide, staring. I remember this is the second dead child he's seen in as many days.

"Is he . . . dead? We should see if there is any ID."

What he means is, *I* should see.

"Fine."

I drop to my knees and rummage in the boy's trouser pockets, front and back, until my hands are drenched and sticky with his blood. There is nothing. I am just about to get up when I notice a corner of card by the opening of his shirt. He seems to be wearing his shirt inside out. I pull out a dog-eared photograph.

The image is of a small family group standing outside a rough Afghan farmhouse. The edges are thumbed and greasy from being touched. Behind them is a jumble of buildings and beyond those a jagged mountain peak rises into a cloudless sky. In the foreground a young girl and boy are playing. They aren't looking at the camera and I can't really make out either of their faces. Just beyond them, near the whitewashed house, is a woman wearing a traditional Afghan tunic dress. She seems to be laughing. I guess that the photographer must have been the boy's father. This was Farshad's family. The young boy in the photo is him, but some years ago. With a pang, it dawns on me why he was wearing his shirt inside out — so the photograph in the breast pocket would lie over his heart.

I take it to show Chip. "This is all he has."

"Someone might be able to ID him."

I turn the photograph over. There's some writing on the back scrawled in pencil. It's a neat, feminine hand. To my surprise it is in English: *My angel. Keep this near your heart and remember me.* It is as though it was written by someone who knew she wasn't going to see Farshad again, someone who loved him. Perhaps his mother? The woman in the photo? Underneath it are three words I don't understand — *Sabz-e Dirang.*

I place the photo carefully back in the dead boy's shirt pocket and tell Chip, trying to keep my voice steady, "I think this should stay right here — where it belongs."

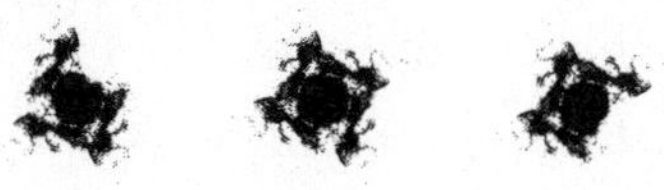

When we get back outside, a small crowd of frightened onlookers have emerged from their houses. The rest of the platoon is here and I can see Gizmo and Jug at a house opposite talking to one of the villagers. Heidi is with Hammed and an elderly Afghan man. She must be trying to find out who the village elders are and what they know. Already, Heidi has got Greg and Jug clearing up some of the debris and is speaking calmly to a couple of the more irate villagers while Hammed translates for her.

I have to admit that she is impressive when she takes control of a situation, and when I remember how I felt a few minutes ago in that room with the girl and Farshad's twisted body I wonder if it's too many tours of this place that have soured her. Maybe I'm the one with the problem. I'm too quick to judge sometimes. It was almost shocking to see how tired she looked when the Americans arrived.

The old man is yammering back at Hammed and he is interpreting when he can get a word in. "Says he see uniforms . . . Afghan security."

"He must be mistaken. The Afghan security forces are working with us — we would know if they were in the area," Heidi says. "Ask if he's sure. Was it the Taliban?"

Hammed asks, but the guy is already shaking his head at the mention of the Taliban. When the old man has said his piece, Hammed tells Heidi, "Is sure. Not Taliban — Afghan security. That is what he say."

"Ask him who they were shooting at."

There is a brief exchange. The old man looks worried, but when Hammed prompts him he says more and points at the house where Chip and I had just been.

"Wild children from mountains. He says village feed them. Sometimes they sleep in empty house."

When Heidi follows the sweep of his arm she sees us. The professional mask drops and her nose wrinkles. "Nice work, Chip," she says sarcastically, without even acknowledging my presence. "I thought I said not to go in."

"It's not his fault," I tell her.

Now she looks at me. "Well, isn't that a surprise? Doing your job so well I can't pick holes? I thought you'd learned something from the IED yesterday. Obviously I was wrong. Back up, Nielson. You're not a private army, you're part of a team, so start acting like it. Now, where's the casualty?"

I am just about to open my mouth and explain what has happened when Chip butts in. "He didn't make it," he tells her flatly, with the briefest glance in my direction.

"I'm sorry," Heidi sighs, and she does look it. There's that tired look again. "Sorry for both of you. At least it wasn't us who killed him. Nielson, you'd better organize collection of the body." She turns to walk off, then stops, mid-stride. "He? Didn't you radio that it was a girl, Chip?"

"Nope," Chip lies, with another look in my direction.

He's covering my back. Probably thinks I'm an idiot, or maybe even that I imagined the girl. I would have told Heidi the truth, but now Chip's made it impossible.

Heidi's eyes narrow and she turns them on me.

"Definitely male," I confirm after glaring at Chip. "Multiple entry wounds. You must have misheard."

She's too busy to argue and strides off, with Hammed in tow.

When we regroup, it becomes clear why Heidi was too preoccupied to bother with us. Yugi is guarding a glowering Afghan boy by the town gates. A prisoner. The lad's age is difficult to guess, but I'd say he's not in his teens yet. His face is round and brown, topped with black, matted hair, and his clothes are little more than rags, torn and stained with God knows what. This is one of the kids who have been giving us so much grief. What was it Farshad called them? The Young Martyrs. He doesn't look much more than a street urchin. Over Yugi's shoulder is the boy's confiscated weapon — an old Kalashnikov, like Farshad's.

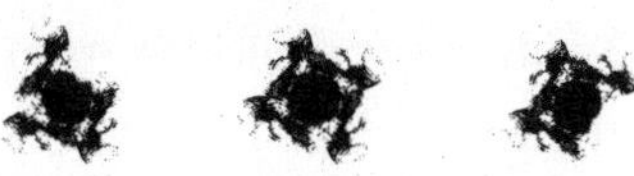

We return to the base early because of the captive. It's almost four o'clock and the sun doesn't go down until seven so there's still enough daylight left to get a little R&R. The boy causes a stir, but it dies down quickly because there's no way the powers that be will give out any more info on him to the likes of us. Besides, most of the platoon prefer to geek out on the Americans and their gear. I swear, if anyone else tells me how great their M4 guns are and how many attachments you can clip to the stupid things I won't be responsible for my actions.

Jug is already in the compound behind the generators, scrubbing his fatigues in a bowl of soapy water when I arrive to do mine. It's the place where everyone does their washing. Staying clean is one of the most important things a soldier can do.

"You seen the SEALs yet?" he asks. "Only I heard their lieutenant is only twenty-three — the youngest marine ever to reach the rank. And in the SEALs, too, that's really something. Those guys are ripped, Buffy — seriously, you'll appreciate it. Go check out the gym."

"I'll pass," I tell him, filling my bowl, even though I'm as keen to see them as anyone. I wonder about the guy with the baseball cap and tattoo. "Seriously, you lot are only interested in the size of their guns and how many Taliban they've whacked."

He laughs, falling silent when he watches me scrunch my dirty trousers into the bowl and scrub at them. The water turns red. And my fingers feel sticky when I pull my hands out. I just stare at them.

"Here," Jug says, pulling my bowl away. "Take a break. I'll do those for you."

I don't argue. Suddenly I need to get away from here. Far away. But who am I kidding? There's nowhere to go. I brace myself for Heidi's cold shoulder and slowly make my way back to our quarters.

The last two days have been intense — draining. If I allow myself to think about things too much I'll be a wreck. No question. Kids are dying, for God's sake. I wonder if they'll even hear about it on the news back home. Somehow I doubt it. Thinking about Mum, Dad, and Jake watching the TV makes me homesick. I want to write a letter home before crashing for the night, but I have no idea what to say. All I can give them is a sanitized picture anyway: *I went on patrol today. I'm tired, but I'm coping. Don't worry. It's not as bad as you think. Blah blah blah . . .* I will tell them I've treated a casualty though. I need to get it off my chest. I'll just leave out his age.

But it's hard to write anything when you're sharing bunk space with the Grinch. I can't relax. Last night Heidi made it pretty clear that the sink was her territory. I left my toothbrush and soap on it and found them stuffed into the top of a pair of used socks this morning. Now one of my primary goals is to learn what winds her up and make sure that I don't do it. I don't want to give her the satisfaction.

I am nearly back at my quarters and dealing with the rising dread when Chip rounds the corner of our building and almost knocks me off my feet.

"Where's the fire?" I smile, hoping for another delay before facing Heidi for the night.

"Not now, Buffy. I'm not in the mood," he growls without stopping. "Not in the bloody mood, OK?"

He disappears without even looking back.

When I get back to my room, Heidi is looking out of the window. If I didn't know better I could swear that her shoulders shudder slightly. It is a moment or two before she turns around. It's a shock. She looks devastated. She's pale and her eyes are bloodshot.

"Everything all right, Corporal?" I ask. "I just saw Chip."

She gives me a guilty look, like I've caught her in bed with him. Then she rummages in her things, digs out a baseball cap, and pulls it over her head so that her eyes are in shadow. *There is no way that Chip would . . . surely?*

"Since you ask, no," she says, falling back onto her bunk. "Everything is not all right. I was just getting my head sorted and now G.I. Joe and the cavalry breeze in. I swear, if McQueen asks me to work with Ben Jackson I'll put in for a transfer . . ." I'm shocked to see a tear rolling from the corner of her eye, but she blinks it away angrily. "Anyway, why should you care if everything's all right?"

I hold up my hands and throw myself on my bed. "Forget I asked." She's obviously got a problem with the Americans. Is Ben Jackson the lieutenant? Maybe she just doesn't want to bow and scrape to someone so young.

"What was Chip doing here?" I press.

"Chip's a moron," she mutters.

It crosses my mind that Chip might have been here defending

me, but the thought of those two being an item is too good to give up.

"And while we're on the subject of morons," she continues provocatively, "don't ever think you can treat me like one."

I sit up and stare at her blankly. "I'm sorry?"

"On the radio today, Chip reported a casualty. A girl."

"You saw the body evacuated, Heidi. It was quite clearly a —"

Heidi does not let me finish the lie. "Whatever. Wearing a blue dress, was she? Black hair, short on words?"

She's got me and she knows it. I wonder if Chip has told her, until I remember he was the one who created the stupid lie.

"I thought so." Heidi looks weary. She sits up again with her back to me and starts to unlace her boots.

There is a silence.

When Heidi speaks again, she doesn't look up and her tone is serious. "Keep away from her," she says. "She is dangerous."

"What do you mean?" I ask. "She's just a young girl." But I'm not sure I believe my own words. Did I really see her get shot, or is this place toying with my sanity?

Heidi doesn't answer at first, just turns around and looks at me long and hard. Then she says, "You've been warned."

10

FOR THE NEXT FEW DAYS THE CONVERSATION WITH Heidi festers in my mind like it is going sour in the heat. The Americans have gone out on some reconnaissance mission and there's nothing else to think about. It's the most she's ever said to me. Frustratingly, it's what she didn't say that is most tantalizing. How would she have any knowledge of this weird Afghan girl, and why wouldn't she share it if the girl is so dangerous? After all, if Heidi knows something, she could compromise our safety by not telling us. I can't stop thinking about it. And now I keep remembering the girl's words to Farshad — *Salāmun alaykum* . . . At least, I think that's what she said. Was it Pashto? I can't ask Hammed — but maybe McQueen would know. I so need to change his opinion of me and this could be the best chance I ever have. All he's had to date is whatever poison Heidi has been dripping into his ear.

It's going to be my new mission. I go looking for the captain but he's nowhere to be found. By the time I go past the rear of the rickety lockup where I know McQueen's keeping the boy we captured, I'm ready to give up. That's when I hear his voice. Bingo. All I need to do is to go back the way I came, through the central compound and past the crappers to a small cleared area where the empty ammo boxes are stacked. I'm about to get going when I catch the captain saying, "Dang it, Hammed, slow down. I'm not that fluent. And keep calm — I don't want you intimidating him."

So I stop where I am to listen. There's a tiny gap in one of the wooden slats and I can see the boy sitting with his back to the side wall. McQueen is farthest from me, a silhouette in the doorway, and Hammed must be at the back wall nearest me because he keeps moving and blocking my view. I feel sorry for the lad — the men must seem quite intimidating to him even though they don't mean to be.

Hammed says, "I was asking where is his family."

The kid rattles off some more Pashto and Hammed starts to shout, but stops himself. The boy yells at them both for a while. Then I hear him crying and McQueen says, "OK, OK, I get it — you don't like the bloody Americans." Then, "I can't believe this, Hammed. The Taliban aren't getting enough people killed so they throw suicidal kids at us now?"

Hammed just grunts.

"Ask him how many of them there are and where the hell they got hold of the Kalashnikovs."

Hammed's voice rumbles angrily and he gets more cheek from the kid. His shadow flies across my peephole and I see the kid scurry to the door, where McQueen catches him before he can escape. It looks like Hammed was intent on giving the kid a pasting. There's a silence and Hammed growls, "He insulted my mother."

"So I gathered. I'll bet he had a few words to say about mine, too. Remind me, how do I ask him whose side he's on?"

So Hammed yammers something at McQueen and to my surprise the captain asks the kid in his own language. It sounds like a pretty good attempt.

The boy answers.

Then McQueen says to Hammed, "Am I hearing this right? Did he say they're not on any side?"

Hammed says, "Correct."

"So they'd happily kill the Taliban as well as us?"

This time the kid replies in English, and it sends shivers down my spine. "We kill all murderers," he says. "Will fight until earth is rid from you."

What is that, some kind of motto? *We kill all murderers*. It's exactly what Farshad told me.

"You speak English, do you?" McQueen sounds surprised. "How about that, Hammed? Well we can't go around shooting at children even if you are pointing Russian assault rifles at us. I need to think about this . . . It's got to go higher. Much higher."

I hear the captain getting up to leave so I race round the blast-bag corridor to try to cut him off. There isn't any need. When I get to the front of the base I find him leaning on one of the armored trucks, taking long draws on a battered cigarette. He stands up when he notices me approach.

"Nielson," he greets me wearily, "I was just thinking about you."

I'm genuinely surprised. "You were?"

He takes a final drag and flicks his stub at the floor, grinding the glowing embers with his boot until they fade to black. He blows the smoke away from me out of the corner of his mouth. Touching. "You're female," he states, gathering his thoughts.

I don't know whether to be offended. "Yes, sir. Last time I looked in the mirror."

"Quite. I'm sorry — I was just thinking aloud. I have a problem and you might be able to help me."

For a moment I am really worried. In training, this was how most of the guys started conversations when they wanted me to help them with girl trouble. I really don't want McQueen to tell me stuff like that. Please God no.

"You know about the captive?"

I hope my relief isn't too obvious. "I was with the team that brought him in, sir."

"Silly of me," he mutters as he feels behind his ear and takes out another crumpled cigarette. I wait patiently while he rummages in his shirt pocket for the silver lighter and flicks the top back to ignite it. He breathes the smoke away from me and watches as it is drawn over his shoulder by the light breeze. "The thing is, Hammed is a bit heavy-handed and I'm too much of an authority figure."

"Sir?"

"He seems to speak English. And he might feel less intimidated with someone closer to his own age. I wonder if you might try talking to him — see if you can draw him out."

This is way out of my comfort zone. "I don't know, sir."

"Oh." The captain's face drops and his cigarette has gone out. He relights it with an irritated flick.

However, I am smart enough to realize this is a chance to put the warning behind me. "But I'm willing to give it a try."

"Good." McQueen smiles, exhaling another white cloud. "So far as we can tell, there's a gang of boys on the loose, terrorizing the area. They seem to be shooting at anything that moves. We don't know for certain yet, but it looks like that gun battle in Darzab was between them and Afghan security, although what on earth Afghan security were doing out here without informing us is anybody's guess. They're supposed to be on our side. I'm waiting for an explanation from Kabul. They might have been on covert ops and got caught out by these infernal kids the same way we were. It's a bloody mess . . . But I digress."

I try not to smile; only McQueen would use words like *infernal* and *digress*.

"See if you can find out where they got hold of their weapons and how many of them there are. You can use my office. You shouldn't be overheard there."

For a moment I think he knows I listened in. But it's just paranoia.

"Get the boy and meet me there in half an hour."

"Yes, sir. But why not ask Corporal Larson? She's female, too," I add cheekily.

The captain rolls the smoldering cigarette between his thumb and forefinger and taps off a gray, crumbling column of ash. "How can I put this? I need someone a little less threatening and a lot more feminine. And younger. Oh — and if Hammed starts asking questions, refer him to me. I'm going to see if he can find someone to look after the boy when you're done."

"Thank you, sir." There is one of McQueen's long silences as I try to phrase what I have come to ask. "I wonder if you could do me a favor in return, sir?"

His eyebrows travel up a notch. Privates don't usually ask captains for favors. "What do you want?"

"Can you tell me what '*Salāmun alaykum*' means?"

McQueen looks at me with a question in his eyes. "Why do you need to know?"

"Research, sir."

McQueen looks impressed. "I'm glad to see you're making an effort. I've been somewhat concerned by the reports Corporal Larson has given me recently."

I can't help sounding hurt. "Sir?"

McQueen looks uncomfortable. I think he's just realizing she may have an agenda. "Never mind. Just keep a low profile for a while, eh?"

I'm so mortified I can't even frame a reply. Heidi has fed him poison and he's fallen for it. I try to keep my voice level when I reply. "Yes, sir."

"And you've got that phrase wrong. It's '*As-Salam Alaykum*' and it means 'peace be with you.' You say it when you greet someone. '*Salāmun Alaykum*' is from the Qur'an and it's only used by the angels when they welcome the dead into paradise."

11

I THINK ABOUT MCQUEEN'S TRANSLATION AS I MAKE my way to the lockup. I have no idea what to make of it. The girl knew Farshad was dying, so maybe she quoted the Qur'an to comfort him? I don't even want to think about the other option. Angels welcoming the dead into paradise? Not now. Not if I want to stay sane — which I most definitely do. The best thing is to put it out of my mind. McQueen hasn't been studying the language long — maybe he's mistaken.

The captured boy is being held in a rickety old lean-to with a warped wooden door secured with a padlock. The only light in there filters through the cracked timbers and holes in the rusting tin roof. Outside, looking like he could happily strangle someone, Jug is on sentry duty. He is squatting with a piece of crumpled paper spread out on his knee and a ballpoint pen in his hand, and he's alternately writing, swearing, and scribbling.

A pained smile flicks across his flushed face when he sees me. "Buffy, I don't s'pose you've got a pen that works?"

"Sorry."

"Sod it." He stands up, angrily scrunches his letter into a ball, and throws it onto a pile of rubble. "It's no good. I can't tell Jenny any of the stuff we do here. She'll miscarry. Oh well, only another hour and a half and some other poor bugger will have to take over."

"Just tell her you're safe and you can't wait to see her."

"That's not bad. Hey — if I wrote, could you dictate some comforting girl stuff for me?"

"No, Jug, I can't. Your wife would notice — believe me. Anyway, McQueen's sent me for the kid."

Jug laughs. "Good luck. I can't get a word out of him. The only reason I know he's still in there is by looking through the holes in the door." He's about to fish in his pocket for the key, then stops. "Before you go in," he adds, lowering his voice. "Some of the guys are saying you saw the girl — you know, when Yugi almost copped it."

"Yeah, we did."

Jug sucks in a breath and shakes his head. "About fourteen, was she? Blue dress? She's bad news, that one."

"C'mon, Jug, it's just some Afghan kid. How can she be bad news?"

"Heidi told me about her on our last tour here. Never saw her myself, but apparently she's always nearby when something bad is about to happen or someone's about to kick the bucket."

I try not to let it show, but his words make my heart race. For a second I'm not sure how to respond. All I'm sure of is that superstition about things like this never ends well, so I poke him in the ribs and make a joke of it. "Get a life, Jug. What do you want to do, hunt her down and burn her at the stake?"

He shrugs. "There's something about her that's not" — he pauses, trying to think of the right words — "of this world." He unlocks the door.

Inside, the kid is playing with some sort of metal toy. He pockets it with lightning speed when the door opens, as if Jug is about to nick it, then spits on the floor. When I enter he stands and looks me up and down like he can't believe that he's looking at a girl in camouflage pants and combat boots.

The boy's silent appraisal of me stops when he realizes I'm looking him in the eye. "Do you have a name?" I ask.

The boy hesitates, then nods. "Name is Husna."

"OK, Husna" — I hold out my hand, but he doesn't take it — "how'd you like to get some air? You're coming with me."

With a painfully superior expression, Husna sticks his chest out and strides past me into the courtyard beyond.

He waits for me to catch up when he realizes he has no idea where I'm intending to take him. He looks so small as he falls into step beside me. It is hard to believe that he was carrying a Kalashnikov only a few days ago. The boy is painfully thin, malnourished, and wearing clothes that look like they have been lived in for years. They are stained black with something. Who am I kidding? I know it has to be blood. The question is, whose?

As we walk through the compound toward McQueen's office, I can't help thinking back to that upstairs room and Farshad's photograph. I begin to wish that I had kept it or at the very least looked at it a little more closely. Husna has got to know something about the boy and his family.

I'm looking at his taut, hunched shoulders and wondering how on earth I'm going to win his trust enough to ask him about it when the American Humvees roll back into the compound. Their reconnaissance mission must be over. I wonder what they were looking for. Husna coughs a ball of foamy saliva onto the packed ground at his feet and rattles off a string of angry sentences in Pashto.

"Do you really have to do that all the time?" I say. "It's disgusting." I stifle a laugh when I realize I sound just like my mother.

Husna shoots me a sheepish look. He almost looks apologetic.

"You're not so big without your machine gun, are you?"

As we start walking again the American with the baseball

cap emerges from one of the Hummers. He adjusts the cap and smiles in our direction. I'm not sure if it's at me or the kid, but I can feel myself coloring up when I glimpse his tattoo again, and I don't know where to look or whether to smile back. Then he's turned away and I kick myself because now he'll just think I was being rude. I hear him ask one of his guys to find McQueen and request a more permanent location for the Humvees. He must be the lieutenant. It looks like the Navy SEALs are going to be staying here for a while, and for some reason the news makes me smile.

When we get to the captain's office, I tell McQueen that he's about to have a visitor, just in case he doesn't want them to overhear my interview with Husna.

"Typical," he mutters with a heavy sigh. "They were supposed to be here the day after tomorrow for a week — tops. Instead of which they arrive ahead of schedule, and then expect to stick around indefinitely. If they'd kept to the timetable, I'd have sorted something out by now. Well, I'd better go and find somewhere for them to set up shop." Then, as he gets up and lifts aside the tarpaulin door, he adds with a nod in Husna's direction, "I'll leave you to it."

"Looks like it's just you and me, then," I tell Husna once McQueen has left, looking around the room and locating a small kettle and a couple of grubby, tannin-stained mugs. "D'you want anything to drink?"

Husna still regards me with intense suspicion, but when he sees the old tobacco tin full of white sugar lumps, his eyes widen and he demands imperiously, "Want tea. Four sugar."

I laugh. "I'll bet you do. You can have a tea with two sugar." A gun-toting kid with a sugar rush? I'm not even going there.

Husna shrugs and tries out McQueen's chair while I make the drinks. I realize that he is looking for something to play with, like any kid his age. But McQueen is too uptight to have anything frivolous knocking around. He gets out his battered toy and spins it on the desk.

It's a dented cylinder with a steel ring around the middle. He holds both ends and sets it spinning on its side. While I'm thinking how to begin, I watch it wobble noisily to a halt. "How old are you, Husna?"

The boy counts on his fingers and shows me. He does not know the English number. "This?"

"Eleven. You are eleven. My name's Elinor — you can call me Ellie." I hold out my hand.

He does not take it. Instead the boy's face wrinkles like there is a bad smell in the room. I try not to take it personally. After all, you can't wipe out hundreds of years of sexist brainwashing just like that. I watch his enormous brown eyes scan the room.

"My brother is two years older than you. He's into computer games, guitars, and football."

"Computer? Farshad's mother have Apple Mac."

Now I'm surprised on way too many levels. All my preconceptions about Afghanistan are wiped out with that one sentence. He knows what I mean by a computer game, and someone he knows has a computer. It's unusual to find electricity out here, let alone to have anything to plug into it. Judging by the landscape in Farshad's photograph, his parents live in the mountains, so that means they must have a generator and be rich by Afghan standards. And Farshad is dead — the boy probably has no idea . . .

"Husna . . ."

He's watching my lips move, won't meet my eyes.

"Your friend Farshad was killed in Darzab. I found him."

Husna's eyes don't even flicker. "I know," he says.

"Do you want to talk about it?"

But he shakes his head. He's clearly not going there.

I grab a couple of tea bags and find myself surprised by the aroma that hits me. Suddenly I'm in the kitchen back home, wondering if I'm the first one up.

Before I can get myself together Husna changes the subject and asks me, "Who does brother support?"

"Man U."

Husna is about to spit again until he sees the reprimand on my face. "Liverpool is better team," he says.

"Exactly what I keep telling him. Whenever we have a kickabout I'm Liverpool, he's Manchester. Most times I have to let him win or he'll sulk. Jake's not a good loser."

Husna crosses his arms. He looks at me, appalled. "Is not right that girl play football."

Now I'm in angry-sister mode. It's like Jake's standing

there giving me grief. "And it's not right for a boy your age to go round pointing guns at people."

"Husna is not boy," he retorts. "Is man."

"Sure you are." I can't help being snarky, but Husna seems to miss it. It's just as well. I don't want to sour the interview before it's even begun so I take a moment to stir the powdered milk and sugar into our muddy drinks with an old pencil. When I'm done, I hold the mug out until he unfolds his arms and takes it. Then I lean against the desk at his side.

"Thank you," he says pleasantly enough.

I return a guarded, "You're welcome," and we both take a sip in silence while I'm thinking, *What now?*

Husna looks at me over the rim of his mug and blows on his drink to cool it. Steam rises in front of his face. "Ellie, you should not let brother win," he says. "If he can't beat girl, is crap player."

I almost spray him with a mouthful of tea. When I manage to swallow, I say, "Underneath that hard shell you're quite a joker, aren't you?"

"What is *joker*?"

"Never mind." I decide it is time to get Husna to open up. "I know you've got no reason to trust me but I'd like to know why Farshad died. Who you were fighting and why."

Husna slurps a mouthful of tea. He does not answer.

"You're not going to tell me?"

He shrugs.

"Don't you think it's important? We could help you. I don't ever want to see anything like that again. A kid his age shot to pieces . . ."

"Then get out from Afghanistan."

"That's your answer?"

As Husna doesn't look like he is about to elaborate any further I change tack. "There was a girl there — with Farshad. I guess that means that she is part of your Young Martyrs club, too?"

"You see Aroush?"

That's what Farshad said to her. It is her name, then. And Husna seems surprised that I should have seen her there.

"Yes, she was there," I tell him. "What is she, some kind of lookout? If so, she's not very good. She's almost got herself killed twice now."

"Not lookout." Husna draws another noisy sip of his tea and his body relaxes. "No girls in Young Martyrs."

"None at all?"

The boy looks at me like I'm an idiot.

"Girls from village go to Farshad's uncle in Pakistan."

"Why?"

Either he doesn't hear my question or he doesn't want to tell me. "Aroush not go with them. Now just follow us. Is good luck — messenger of Allah."

"A messenger of Allah?"

Husna nods and I wait for an explanation. But that's all he's offering. He ignores me and starts clicking one of the pens on McQueen's desk.

"Is she from the same place as the rest of you?"

Husna shrugs again. "Farshad's sister. Was born when Farshad is two year old. Father, Jahadar, was from Afghanistan, mother from decadent West."

"Is that so?" That makes sense, but I can't believe my ears. I think I'm actually making progress. Farshad's mother is from the West! So that explains why she has a computer. I think of the photo again, the woman in Afghan clothes outside the whitewashed house. "His parents need to know what's happened to him. Do you know how I can find them?"

Husna looks away from me.

I take it that he will only speak about the girl right now. "What did you mean when you said Aroush is good luck?"

The boy fiddles with his cup before seeming to come to a decision. "She was in schoolroom when planes come. Direct hit."

Aroush survived a missile impact? I can't begin to imagine the trauma she must have been through. "That doesn't sound very lucky, Husna."

"She survive. We all see her in mountains."

"But the planes? What planes? Why was your village bombed?"

Husna is sullen again. His eyes fill up, but nothing comes.

I feel like I may be treading on a nerve so I try another tack. "OK, so tell me about the Young Martyrs. Are you all from the same village?"

Now Husna clams up as if he is worried that he has told me too much. His head drops and he won't make eye contact. I resist the urge to lift his chin and make him. So the boy doesn't completely trust me yet, why should he? I wait patiently while Husna swills what's left of his tea. The interview is over. I'm no child psychologist, but it's obvious that this boy has seen stuff no one his age should ever see. He needs time before he's going to open up.

"I'm only asking you all this because I want to help," I say. "You get that, don't you? Your friends, the Young Martyrs, should be in school, not playing with guns."

He ignores me, scanning the room again, and I realize why.

"Hungry?"

He nods.

"C'mon, then, let's get you something to eat." I'm thinking maybe food will help. The kid looks like he hasn't eaten a square meal in days. "We'll go and see what they've got in the canteen."

But before either of us has a chance to move, there is the sound of lighthearted banter outside. American accents. The tarpaulin lifts and two guys duck under it. The baseball-cap lieutenant and another SEAL with dark hair and olive skin. Three stripes on his sleeve, so he's a sergeant.

Husna backs away, suddenly tense again. I can feel hatred oozing from him and my body tingles with adrenaline because of it. If the kid still had his gun, I'm sure the two guys would be dead by now.

The lieutenant is still in fatigues, dusty from days on the road. As he takes his cap off and runs his fingers through his hair his eyes sparkle. They widen almost imperceptibly when I stand up.

The sergeant gives me an approving look. "And you said there was no scenery in Helmand, Lieutenant!" His accent is Hispanic.

I put myself between the Americans and Husna, mortified. "Please — you need to leave." I'm trying to keep calm, but I feel like any progress I made with the boy could go down the drain if the sergeant doesn't stop joking and get a million miles away from us. "Captain McQueen asked me to interview the prisoner in private."

"Beautiful and feisty — just how I like 'em," the sergeant continues, like he's not heard a word I've said.

The lieutenant elbows him. "OK, Carlos. We respect that, Private . . . ?"

"Nielson, sir."

"Private Nielson — good to meet you. I'm Lieutenant Jackson, and I apologize on behalf of my sergeant here. He'll be much better behaved when he's had some shut-eye. If you bump into your captain, tell him we need to see him about where he'd like us to set up camp."

I feel like I'm holding on to a scream.

Husna must be, too. Something in him seems to snap — it's almost audible. Before I can get myself in between them he's hurling himself over the captain's desk and at the lieutenant, scattering pens, cups, and maps, and yelling, "YOU KILL THEM! KILL THEM ALL!"

12

JACKSON IS ALMOST BOWLED OVER BY THE FEROCity of Husna's attack. The boy is landing blows and kicks on him and trying to make a grab for the pistol holster on his belt. But an eleven-year-old is no match for a Navy SEAL. The American lifts him from the floor, rotates the boy round in his arms, and pins him, still kicking and swearing, against his chest. "Take it easy, buddy — what are you talking about?"

His sergeant just stands there, looking bemused.

I'm torn between my concern for Husna and anger at the visitors. Unless I get the boy away from them I'll never get any more information from him. If they hadn't barged in with their stupid banter, none of this would have happened.

"LET GO!" Husna screams.

I try to speak calmly and evenly. "Sir, you have to let him go."

Husna gives up the fight and goes limp in the lieutenant's arms, wracked with sobs.

"Please!" I yell, forgetting myself. "Sir — just give me a minute with him and we'll get out of your way."

Slowly the American lowers him to the ground, and Husna lies there, crying.

Jackson raises his arms in mock surrender. He looks taken aback, almost hurt. As if Husna were some Western kid taking a dislike to him for no reason. "That's just what we were about to do." He lifts the tarpaulin again. "Sergeant . . ."

As soon as the tarp falls behind them I haul Husna to his feet. "You OK?" I am shaking as I grab his shoulders. I've never shouted at a superior officer before.

Husna does not reply. He turns his bloodshot eyes on me. I think he is embarrassed about falling apart and I'm stressed out by the whole episode. My head is pounding. Somehow I've got to calm down, go out there, and walk past the Americans as if I know what I'm doing. I'm hoping they don't say anything. I want to ask Husna what the hell that was about, but he's not ready to tell me yet. Nowhere near. After this drama I'd be surprised if he ever will.

Finally I manage to pull myself together. "Look, we're going to walk out of here, but before you spit in their faces, just remember they're ordinary people just like you and me, right? Now, you're going back to the lockup, but it's only until Hammed can decide what he's going to do with you."

His face drops. "I want stay with you."

I try to hide my emotions as I push aside the tarpaulin — relief and anguish flood my chest in equal measure. He still trusts me, thank God. But I'm a soldier and a medic, not a social worker, and he can't rely on me forever. I'm hit with a huge wave of guilt. How can I do anything but let him down?

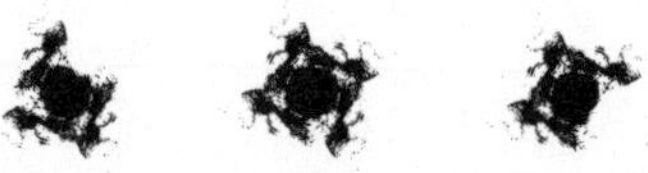

The captain meets us as Husna and I emerge into the late-afternoon sun. The Americans are nowhere to be seen. McQueen is rolling another cigarette between his yellowed fingers. The paper tears so he gives up on it, brushing the remains off his hands petulantly.

"Sir, the Americans . . ." I begin.

"Yes, yes, I know — parked their bloody Humvees by the generator. Come back and see me when you've deposited your friend." McQueen forces a smile for Husna's sake and carries on to his office, muttering loudly to himself.

When I get Husna back to the lockup, Jug is still there waiting for us. He springs to his feet. From the way his face falls I guess he thought I was the relief guard. Then I hit on another great idea for bonding with my charge.

"Hey, I'm thinking we could play football sometime. Are you up for it, Husna?"

Husna makes a face. "With you?"

"Cheeky. Did I mention that I was the Football Association UK's Under-16s Striker of the Year?"

I can almost hear the cogs whirring in Husna's brain. He's thinking about it.

"You're a dark horse, Buffy," Jug says. "Maybe we should clear it with the captain first?"

He is afraid the boy will do a runner. "Come on, Jug, it's a secure compound. But if it will make you feel any better I'll ask McQueen."

"Nah — I'll do it. Count me in. Yugi's got a ball."

"I play with her," Husna tells Jug urgently as he is hustled into his prison. "Ellie is footballing champion."

"Then I'll be with you two as well," Jug tells him.

"Not a champion," I tell them, feeling the weight of expectation. "Striker of the Year."

Jug chuckles. "It's about time we had someone to put bloody Wayne Rooney in his place."

"Wayne Rooney?"

"Wayne Ritchie, actually. A bighead who goes round telling everyone he tried out for Man U."

"And did he?"

"Who knows? He's good, but he lies like a trooper, if you'll pardon the pun. Full of himself."

"Don't you mean *swears* like a trooper, Jug?"

"If you say so. He does both and he's still a prat."

Great. Defeat in a game with this Ritchie guy is really going to help my relationship-building plans with Husna. I say my good-byes and head off to see McQueen. The Americans are back in his office now. Lieutenant Jackson is reclining in the only other chair, his feet propped on the corner of McQueen's desk. There's a couple of days' shadow on his chin. His hair is bleached by the sun so the stubble's not too dark. And he's dead gorgeous. From the self-assured twist of his mouth, I'd say he knows it, too. Not my type though. Definitely not. Not that anyone joins the army looking for love.

I let the tarpaulin fall behind me and walk over to the opposite corner of the captain's desk. Carlos has located an upturned box and is sitting on it. Captain McQueen sits between them, behind his desk, like a rabbit caught in headlights. He seems relieved to see me.

"Nielson — we were just talking about you."

"Sir?"

The corner of the lieutenant's mouth lifts slightly. "I was telling the captain how we barged in on you."

Irritation still churns in my chest and my cheeks are beginning to flush. I wonder if he's just playing me. He's obviously amused by the whole situation. I can't calm down. Not yet.

Thankfully, the captain does not seem to notice my mood. "How did you get on with the boy?"

I'm not sure I want to say with the Americans present. Things are balanced on a knife-edge with Husna. I know I can get him to tell me more, but only if I can keep his trust. If he suspects I've been talking to the Americans he'll clam up.

When I hesitate, McQueen glances at Jackson. He's exasperated with me. "It's fine, Nielson. The lieutenant is interested in our young friends."

"The Young Martyrs, right?" Jackson inquires, taking his feet off the desk.

"You've heard of them?"

He's looking right into my eyes as he leans forward and rests his arm on the corner of the desk. "We'd heard reports of wild kids up here, but the name was new to me. Until the captain here told us about your dead boy."

It's crazy, but I'm worried that McQueen has told them about Farshad so soon. I think it's because the memory is still so new for me and there's a nagging worry at the back of my mind because of the way Husna reacts around them. It makes me feel protective. I mean, I know there's no love lost between the Afghans and the Americans but Husna's feelings are extreme and they seem to be so raw. My response is clipped. "They're kids. They have guns. At the moment that's all I know, sir."

"Now, Nielson . . ." McQueen begins, but Jackson silences him with a gesture.

His level of confidence is shocking. McQueen is older and more senior, but you wouldn't think it. Suddenly I'm wondering who I'm reporting to here.

Jackson's gaze is steady. "That's true, Private Nielson, to an extent. Wild kids are one thing; wild kids with guns are another. Wild kids with guns and a name — now I'd say they're something else again, wouldn't you?"

"I don't follow."

"A name means they're organized, that they have a plan, a purpose. They want something and they'll continue to be 'Young Martyrs' until they get it."

It's like he's taken the tangle that was in my head and straightened it all out. For a moment I'm floored. By the look on his face I'd say McQueen is, too. I wait in silence for him to speak again and it is in that moment that I understand the difference between McQueen and Jackson — one is trained to lead and the other is born to it. That's why Jackson is a lieutenant in the Navy SEALs at just twenty-three. No doubt his troops would follow him to the ends of the earth. While I wait for him to speak, I think I might even have stopped breathing.

"Let me tell you where we fit in. We're here to investigate an arms cache in the mountains, and trading over the border to Pakistan. We don't know how, but these mountain kids seem to have got hold of some pretty powerful weapons. I think they're from the cache my team is looking for. Question is, where is it? Yakmak? Quetta? Some other village in the mountains around Sabz? And why aren't the Taliban using them?"

"Sabz?" I say. "Do you mean Sabz-e Dirang?"

Jackson looks at me sharply. "The mountain, yes. You've heard of it?"

"The casualty in Darzab . . . the dead boy, sir, he had a family photo. On the back of it was a message and the words 'Sabz-e Dirang' . . ."

The Americans exchange glances.

McQueen asks, "Was there anything else on it?"

"No, sir. The message was a . . . sentimental one." Although I'm thinking that *sentimental* doesn't feel quite right. More desperate.

"Nice work, Private," Jackson says. "If you ask me, you've just made our job a whole lot easier. It shouldn't be too hard to find out what village Farshad was from. Not now that we have one of his friends in custody. We're going to find that cache and destroy it before some of the rocket launchers in there are used against our guys. Then we're going to disarm your Young Martyrs and make sure that they go to school."

"What if they don't cooperate, sir? From what I've seen these kids are angry and traumatized. They're more likely to shoot at you with semiautomatics."

The lieutenant looks at me evenly. "Well, clearly, it would be unfortunate if we had to shoot back. We'll be trying to negotiate."

Carlos chips in. "Captain McQueen tells us they don't like the insurgents much, either, and they know the area . . ."

"We want them on our side," Jackson finishes.

There's a silence. McQueen takes a bent roll-up from behind his ear and stubs the end on his desk. He says pointedly,

"Private Nielson is already trying to build a relationship with the boy. I'm sure she'll be able to get him to see sense."

It dawns on me what they're getting at. I am horrified. "But, surely . . . you don't mean to use Husna as a guide?"

The lieutenant doesn't answer my question. He's thinking. "I'd like to talk to him myself," he tells McQueen, ignoring me.

Before McQueen has a chance to answer, I square up to the American. It's the first stupid thing he's said. "Sir, I'm not sure that's a good idea."

McQueen bridles, but Jackson holds up his hand. "Why is that, *Private*?"

I stand my ground. "With respect, what are you going to do with him? Cuff him to a chair? You saw how he reacted to you. If you want any more from Husna, you should go through someone he trusts."

"And I guess that would be you?"

"I think he is beginning to trust me, yes. In spite of interruptions."

Lieutenant Jackson smiles at my dig and looks at me in silence for a moment. He rubs his chin thoughtfully. "OK, Private Nielson," he says. "I like people who aren't afraid to tell it as they see it. We'll go through you, but in the meantime, why don't you tell us what Husna's given you so far?"

A wave of relief leaves me feeling almost lightheaded. It's like I've fought in Husna's corner and won. If I can gain his trust and get the information we need, they won't need to use him. And at least Jackson seems to listen to and respect a good argument. That gives me hope. The tension drains from my shoulders like he's just found the tap, and I have to stop myself rewarding him with a grateful smile.

I go ahead and tell him what Husna has said and he listens intently; there is not much he does not already know. But he looks strangely at his sergeant when I tell him that the Young Martyrs are followed everywhere by the girl, Aroush. By the end I can't help wondering how the lieutenant has got me to trust him so readily. I'm new here. Inexperienced. For all I know he could be using me. All I can go on is the fact that I'm usually a good judge of people and the lieutenant seems genuine. But however impressive the guy may seem, I'm not going to be won over that easily. Jackson's going to have to prove himself to me.

The sun has set by the time I get back to my quarters to crash, and Heidi's waiting for me. She's pacing so hard I'm surprised she hasn't worn a groove in the floor, and she looks like she could punch someone.

There are no niceties, no pretense. "So, McQueen asked you to question the boy? I suppose the Americans were there?"

I sit on the side of my bunk, pull off my sweat-soaked T-shirt, and enjoy the cooling sensation. There is no need to answer. She knows.

"Funny how you can be here just a few days and already you've got McQueen and Jackson fawning all over you. What's that about? Have *they* seen you in the buff, too?" Then her voice drops like she's thinking aloud, "Jackson doesn't even know I exist."

I know the minute I open my mouth she'll wipe the floor with me. She outranks me so I keep my mouth shut.

"And McQueen is an idiot. What does he think this is, amateur hour?"

That stings a reply out of me. "He must think I'm the right person for the job. Looks like your little smear campaign has hit a snag."

Heidi covers the space between us faster than I would have thought possible. She almost spits her words into my face. The damp heat of her breath makes me blink. "Don't get smart with me, Nielson." Then something like guilt flickers across her face and she backs off.

"Look" — I'm shaken, but I try not to let it show — "I didn't ask for this, OK? And I had grief from McQueen thanks to you. I don't appreciate you making me look like the camp troublemaker."

She has her back to me now. There is a simmering pause.

"So, did you see the Americans or not?"

"Yes. The lieutenant — Jackson. He asked me to find out more."

Heidi collapses onto her bed and looks at the ceiling, battling with something.

"If it's any consolation, I didn't make a very good impression with *them*, either."

She snorts derisively. "Really? I'd have thought you'd be just his type — young, pretty . . . safe."

I try a softer approach. "Jackson's type? I wouldn't know. And what does that have to do with anything? Seriously, Heidi, what's eating you?"

She covers her head with her hands. It's so unlike her to lose control like this that I'm really shocked.

"He's been here before — Ben. Something bad happened — really bad . . ." Then she whispers, "I'm so sorry . . ."

I'm tempted to go over and put my arm around her shoulder. A sixth sense tells me to resist, but I say, "It doesn't have to be like this you know, you and me. We could be friends."

Silence.

It's a moment before she takes a deep breath and tells me in no uncertain terms, "Not in this life."

There's nothing more to say. I clean my teeth and Heidi cries herself to sleep, or whatever it is she is doing under her pillow, while I lie there in the darkness and try desperately to stop my mind racing.

Husna's desolate sobs echo in my head. I see Yugi standing on the IED, Farshad's broken body, Lieutenant Jackson lifting the tarpaulin door. In the cool of the night, with the rattle of Heidi's sleeping breaths, it takes me ages to fall asleep. At last my eyelids grow heavy and the thoughts that have anchored me in the waking world float away like mist. I see blood, then soapsuds — it's my wash bowl and I'm staring at my bloody trousers, and inside one of the pink bubbles the strange Afghan girl beckons to me, pointing to the mountains just before she takes a bullet that doesn't hurt her. I want to ask her what it all means, but the bubble pops and blackness swallows me so gently and so completely that I don't even notice its approach.

13

I WAKE JUST BEFORE DAWN WITH AN IMAGE BEHIND my eyes. It is of a cratered Afghan village scattered with the bodies of children. I'm wet with sweat yet I can't even remember most of the dream, just the bodies and the feeling of being completely and utterly helpless. My tongue feels like sandpaper. I stumble over to the sink and gulp water straight from the old tap. When I look around Heidi has already gone.

On my way to the canteen for breakfast I see that the Americans have pitched camp a short distance away from their battered, dusty Humvees, which are now parked outside the crappers. It annoys me that McQueen could insult our guests like that, but he probably had nowhere else for them to set up. Six of them, including Lieutenant Jackson, lounge topless in the morning sun outside their tents. Heidi is there talking to Jackson. Maybe trying to find out what I've said. I can't help noticing the curve of his perfectly toned shoulders, the little dent in his neck, but even from where I'm standing it's clear that Heidi can barely look at him. I'm betting that the only reason she's talking to the guy is because McQueen has told her she has to deal with him. For all I know they could be discussing what to do with Husna. Heidi's body language makes me wonder what Jackson could have done that was so bad last time they met. Then I remember Heidi saying *I'm sorry* — and I don't know what to think.

I need to see Husna again, but it'll have to wait. My unit has been ordered to assemble in the courtyard. We're going on another patrol to find out more about the Young Martyrs or where they might be hiding. It's still hot, but there's more of a wind today so I'm not feeling quite so bad under all my gear. I toy with the idea of asking McQueen for a day off patrol to speak with our captive, but I don't want to let my unit go out a man short. I can't abandon the guys. When she's done talking to Jackson, Heidi waits at the head of the unit for the all clear from our sentries — Nick and Jimbo — who are in position on the second floor of a bombed-out building near the gates. I sneak a peek at the sunbathing Americans again, then catch the look Heidi throws my way.

Just as I'm beating myself up over my lack of self-control

one of the Americans scrambles to his feet and yells, "INCOMING!"

The whole platoon scatters and dives for cover. In the chaos I just catch a streak of orange shooting over the perimeter wall toward the crappers. The Americans are flying like they've been hit by a bowling ball. Somehow I can't seem to move my feet.

"For God's sake, Buffy!"

It's Chip. He grabs me by the shoulder straps and virtually flings me with him over the circle of sandbags that surround one of our gun emplacements. The explosion that follows us as we fly through the air thuds into my backpack like a sledgehammer, and throws us onto the guys who are already taking cover there. In the jumble of arms and legs I can make out Chip's concerned face twisting in slo-mo and finally we land together on a pile of spent rounds. Somehow I find myself sliding to a halt straddling his chest.

"Not now, Buffy — there's a time and a place . . ."

I can't believe he's joking when we're under rocket attack. Unbelievable.

"INCOMING!"

A second RPG slams into one of the Humvees, and the percussion wave hammers into me and throws me in an almost perfect somersault onto my back. Through the clattering shower of debris that follows, I hear our guys lock onto their targets and open up with mortars and the big machine guns. There is another, smaller explosion as the fuel tank on the stricken Hummer explodes. Through the confusion one shout shocks me like ice water, an American voice.

"I'm hit!"

Another joins in. "Man down! Man down! Medic!"

Chip yanks me to my feet, rubble showering from his back and shoulders, and shouts above the chaos, "Looks like you're up!"

He spins me round by the shoulders to face the spot where I had last seen Lieutenant Jackson and his troops relaxing, and I locate the casualty — no, two casualties — not far from the burning wreck of the Humvee. Nearby, one of the Americans is sitting up holding his side, and his hands are red with blood. It's the sergeant, Carlos. The other casualty is lying prone where he has fallen. With horror I realize that it is Hammed.

I scramble over the sandbags, fumbling in my pack for my trauma dressings, and finding that my mind is suddenly blank. It seems like all my training is being sucked into a black hole in my head and all I have to rely on is instinct.

The American is upright and breathing, holding his side. A quick visual tells me that the bleeding does not look excessive. But Hammed, a few meters away, is not moving. I have to treat him first.

I call across to Carlos, "I'll just be a second — OK? Keep pressure on it." His breathing is shallow from the pain, but he manages a smile.

I arrive at Hammed's side, throw down my backpack, and drop to my knees, looking around to locate Heidi as the other medic. She's near the gates about a hundred meters away and running in my direction, back toward the casualties. Behind her a third flash of orange is falling from the sky like a thunderbolt — and it's heading right toward both of us.

"BUFFY!" Yugi has seen the danger and the idiot starts running toward us. Everything seems to slow down, but there is nothing anyone can do. Gizmo tries to grab his sleeve as he passes, but Yugi slips from his grasp and keeps running. God knows what he's thinking.

I only manage to shout a warning at Heidi, "INCOMING! GET DOWN!" before throwing myself on top of Hammed.

Another thudding impact lifts us together and showers us with hot dirt. Shards of metal hammer into my body armor, knocking the wind out of me. My ears are ringing and I can't see for a moment because the dirt scratches my eyes every time I try to open them. Rubbing them with my sleeve just makes it worse. Panic rises in my chest because I can hear the bedlam around me but I'm helpless until I can open my burning eyes. Shaking my head and blinking at the same time, I manage to clear my vision. My eyes are streaming now. I roll over and snort the dirt out of my nose. It's still pouring like water from my helmet and back.

The shooting pain I feel in my back and side makes me think I've been hit, but when I check the tears in my body armor I find with relief that there are shards of metal but that nothing actually made it through. I hope I'm not going to have to pay for my next armor, too. Thank God we were all dressed ready for patrol. My ribs hurt like hell though. I look frantically around and see Heidi getting to her feet and staggering through a cloud of dust to a body lying in a pool of blood. It is Yugi.

I want to scream. I want to swear at him for being so stupid and curse his sorry behind for wasting all my efforts at the IED.

In the same instant I'm praying he is alive.

Heidi is already at his side. She's good at her job, I have to leave her to it, but my heart is going so hard I can feel it in my throat. *Yugi has to live; he has to.*

I wrench my attention back to Hammed. His breathing is fine and he has a pulse — a strong one — but blood is oozing slowly from just behind his right ear. He's been knocked out by a rock or shard of shrapnel, which, fortunately, seems to have ricocheted off his skull. I slide my hands down his sides and start to check his body for any hidden injuries or bleeding. He's out of it, but otherwise unhurt. I roll him into the recovery position — that's all I can do for the moment — before getting to my feet. My next priority is the sergeant, but I can't help but look over at Yugi again. It's just for a second. When I turn back, I find I'm just steps from the lieutenant, who is organizing his men to douse the fire and clear the other two Humvees. Our eyes meet.

He shouts over the noise of our counterattack, "Nielson, how's Carlos?"

I'm mortified. He must think I'm just standing here like a dork. "Just about to check, sir."

His face is serious. "Do your best for him. And I don't want Carlos evacuated unless he's on his last breath."

I am staggered. Do your best? Like I'd do any less? Irritated I say, through gritted teeth, "Yes, *sir*."

He nods and turns his back on me, to check on his other men.

It's ridiculous, after nearly being taken out by a rocket, but I feel hurt. I thought he respected me. Why is he being such an *arse*hole?

I examine the injured sergeant. The Americans were sunbathing. No body armor. Carlos's side is bloody, ragged. As far as I can see, something sharp has passed right through him just below the ribs and about half an inch in. Doesn't look like any of it is left in the wound. And the blood isn't squirting out, but he could be bleeding internally. Suddenly I'm aware of Jackson behind me, watching. I have an opinion and I have to voice it whether the lieutenant likes it or not.

"It doesn't look too bad," I say over my shoulder. "Looks like the shrapnel hasn't hit an artery. But he needs to be evacuated, sir. This man needs specialist help."

"Look again and see what you can do. That's all I'm asking." He doesn't wait for me to argue, turning to give orders to two Navy SEALs armed with mortars. Then he jogs off toward the rattling gun emplacements where McQueen is organizing the counterattack, shouting to me as he runs, "I need him — OK?"

"You shouldn't mind the lieutenant," Carlos tells me as I start to clean the dirt away and dress his wound.

"Shouldn't I?" I press my lips together and concentrate on the task.

"No. He just doesn't want to lose his second in command. And I'm the best explosives expert in the SEALs."

"He may have to lose you."

"I'm not hurt that bad. You said so."

"But I can't say that for certain!"

Carlos ignores this. "I know Ben Jackson better than he knows himself. That counts for a lot when you're putting your life on the line. A leader needs people he can trust to carry the flame if he falls. You get what I'm saying?"

"Loud and clear. You must be very happy together."

Carlos winces as I apply pressure. "And, to tell the truth," he continues, "I don't want to leave, either. Not like this, in some freak accident. What do you say, Doc?"

He talks as though he's cut himself shaving, and I am still aware that while I am here Yugi is badly hurt.

"I'm not a doctor, but it doesn't look too serious," I inform him, only barely aware of my own voice. "Although infection could set in if you don't get it checked out at the field hospital."

While I am tying off the dressing, my eyes seem to lose focus. Everything starts swimming around me like it did when I was treating the dying boy. Black spots and shadows. A rushing wind. I attempt to shake it off, and stop what I am doing to look behind me, irresistibly drawn to where Heidi kneels. Gizmo is next to her, fretting. Black smoke from the burning Humvee interrupts my view every now and again, but with horror I realize she is doing CPR, pumping Yugi's chest with her flattened palms, listening to it, and breathing for him.

As I get to my feet, Heidi stops pounding and falls back on her haunches, exhausted. I run over to them. Yugi's pooling blood is sinking into the earth, the surface layered with settling flecks of Afghan dirt, and the whole puddle is shuddering to the thud of mortars being fired out of the base. I find I'm holding my breath as if waiting for Yugi to rise with a gasp — but it is not going to happen. Everything around me is blurred and indistinct. I'm watching, waiting, not knowing how it all works, how I can feel like I'm losing a part of my own life when I've only known him for a few days. My heart breaks when I think of a letter flying back home to Yugi's family because I see my own parents opening the envelope and for a minute everything seems hopeless. Then the world is in my face again, shaking me by the shoulders.

"Don't stop!" Pushing Heidi aside, Gizmo lays into his friend with desperate, rib-cracking force. I can hear his voice, broken by the effort of telling Yugi to live.

Heidi shakes her head, but lets him try anyway. She looks skyward while she tries to catch her breath and watches the clouds until some sixth sense seems to tell her I am there, because she turns her head and looks at me blankly. That's when I see — over Heidi's shoulder, through the smoke, beyond the gates and the razor wire — a small figure in blue, walking away from the camp, through the ancient olive grove and toward the mountains. Aroush.

Salāmun alaykum, Yugi.

14

I'M WONDERING IF I SHOULD LET JACKSON AND McQueen know. We should stop firing in case we hit the girl. But she's nowhere near where the RPGs were launched, or where the plumes of smoke from our counterattack are rising. Besides, something in my gut tells me that this attack has nothing to do with the Young Martyrs. It's normal, everyday Taliban stuff. For a moment Jug's words about the girl haunt me and I think she might have been there trying to warn me, only I didn't notice her. I shake the thought out of my head. It's more likely that she was trying to find out what we've done with Husna. Isn't it? But she wouldn't have been able to get close enough to the base.

"Stop it, Gizmo, he's gone." Heidi comes out of her daze and lays a hand on Gizmo's huge shoulder.

He doesn't stop. I'm beginning to realize that war messes with your normal emotions. Few tears are shed for the dead. There isn't time. Not even if you've known them for years. The only way to cope, to keep going, is to do. That's why Gizmo continues to pound the hell out of Yugi's lifeless chest, and it's why I decide to make myself busy so that nobody will see the newbie cry. I get on the radio and call for a medevac team. When I'm done I notice Heidi's leg. Her trousers are ripped and bloody.

"Do you need treatment?" I ask her.

Heidi looks at me blankly for a moment, then reads the direction of my gaze. "What? Oh . . . No, I'm fine."

Chip comes skidding to a halt beside us. When he sees Yugi, anguish lances across his face. He looks away.

"What happened?" he manages when he turns around. "Last time I saw him he was on his way toward the gates."

"He took the full force of the RPG in his back," Heidi murmurs. "Saved my life — and probably yours, too," she continues, looking at me. Heidi seems to be fighting her emotions, as if she is angry that Yugi threw himself between me and the blast.

Chip looks skyward. Then he bends down and retrieves the dog-eared deck of cards from the sleeve of Yugi's jacket.

As if this is the final remnant of Yugi's spirit departing, Gizmo stops pumping and gently lifts his friend's lifeless arms and places them across his chest. He gets up as quickly as he arrived. "Best get on, then," he mutters, walking off without another word. Chip jogs after him.

When our counterattack ends and the guns have fallen silent I go back to check on Carlos and Hammed. I'm relieved to find that Hammed has come to and is holding his head. Carlos isn't looking too good though. The color has drained from his face.

"How're you doing?"

"Been better." He manages a smile and tries to sit up, and looks like he's about to hurl.

"Still want to stay?" I ask him as we watch the medevac Black Hawk land inside the gates. I wave to the disembarking paramedics.

Jackson drops by my side without warning. I feel a tingle as his arm brushes against my thigh. Maybe I'm still on edge after the battle. *Get a grip*, I tell myself. *Concentrate on your job.* He takes a quick look at the compression bandage. The white surface is starting to turn pink in the middle. "How're you doing, buddy?"

Carlos won't look at me. "I'm fine. Don't let them take me, Lieutenant, not like this."

Jackson watches for my reaction. "I need him to stay if possible . . . We can evacuate him later if it doesn't heal."

"But, sir, I'm worried about infection. There's a hole in his side, and who knows what went through it with all the crap that those RPGs threw up."

He holds me in his gaze. "I trust you, Private. Look after him. If it gets worse, we'll review the situation, OK?"

I'm not happy, but it's clearly not my decision. All I can do is shrug. *He's your responsibility.*

The paramedics and a doctor arrive at a crouching run with their stretcher. The doctor is a lanky guy with a lined face and a serious expression. By the way he looks at me I can tell he doesn't mess around.

"We've got two casualties," I inform him, "and one KIA." Killed In Action. I want to use Yugi's name, but keep it professional. I convince myself it's not uncaring, just necessary. "Hammed here has a head injury, and this is Carlos — he has a shrapnel wound. He's not to be evacuated."

The doctor looks at me. "Says who?"

"I do."

The doctor looks Jackson up and down, then examines the wound. When he's done, he looks at me. "Did you dress this?"

I nod.

"Nice work." He leaves me to re-dress it and stands to talk with Jackson. "This soldier needs specialist treatment. He's coming to the field hospital."

The lieutenant isn't fazed. He holds out his radio handset. "I need him here for a specific mission. You want to speak to General Macallum about it? We're here on his direct orders."

I recognize the name. Macallum is the new commander of US forces in Afghanistan, the highest of the high. How and why is Lieutenant Jackson reporting to him directly?

The doctor seems to notice Jackson's youth for the first time. He's losing his patience. "You're not on your PlayStation now, son. And I don't care whose orders you're following. This man needs treatment."

Jackson ignores the insult and continues to hold out the phone. "Leave the medic some antibiotics, tetanus, whatever. She'll take good care of him."

That scares me. "But, Lieutenant," I plead, "I'm a medic, not a nurse . . ."

"You'll do fine. The British Army gives you morphine training, doesn't it?"

I can't think of a decent enough argument on the spot. And all this is over my head anyway. I'm just a private. I do what I'm told.

The doctor snatches Jackson's handset and asks if he can talk to whoever's in charge. His jaw drops when an irate, distant voice buzzes in his ear. "Yes, sir," he says, contrite. "Yes, General. I'll make sure he has all the help he needs."

As soon as I can I make my way to Husna's lockup. Normally I'd expect a kid his age to be terrified after hearing a full-scale firefight going on around him, but something tells me this particular kid may be hardened to it all. By the time I get there, I find Jug has decided it's safe to let the boy out to play with his metal toy. He is trying to write his letter again, this time with a chewed, stubby pencil. When he sees me approach he jumps up.

"God, you look awful."

I shake my head. I can feel my hair is matted and filthy. "Thanks. I just came to check if Husna's OK."

"Didn't even bat an eyelid. I'm useless here. I should have been with you guys in the compound. What happened? All I could see was the smoke — and the medevac chopper. We took three hits, didn't we?"

He's waiting for me to tell him about the casualties. For a moment I can't speak.

"Someone bought it?"

I nod. "Yugi. The other two are fine — Hammed and one of the Americans."

"Yugi?" Jug's on his feet, scrunching up his letter and throwing it away. He paces away from me and back again, swearing. When he's let it out, he retrieves his letter and unfolds it like it's suddenly precious to him again, and smoothes it flat against his leg.

I can't help him deal with the grief. I have no words. All I want to do right now is work because that way I can forget, so I just point at Husna and ask, "Do you mind if I have a word?"

"Mind? Help yourself." He points to a pile of sandbags about twenty meters away and gets to his feet. "I'll just go over there and finish this pile of rubbish. A bit of shade will help me get my head together. Hey, I've told Ritchie you're an ace footballer. He says he's going to take you down. And Chip's running bets. He's got half the base putting money on you scoring two goals so we'd better get this match sorted."

"Great," I say to his back, "no pressure, then."

Jug just waves his arm. "We'll do it for Yugi — the Wainwright Memorial Match."

When he's out of earshot, I go and sit cross-legged on the floor next to Husna. He pockets his toy with lightning reflexes. "What is that thing anyway?" I ask him.

He doesn't answer me.

"Are you OK? I came to check. All that noise was a rocket attack. It's over now."

Still no response.

I wait. After a while he rubs his nose on his sleeve and shrugs. I get it. The boy knows an RPG when he hears one. My heart sinks. I wonder if I'm going to have to start from scratch. His toy is obviously out of bounds so I rack my brains and realize that the best subject to get him to open up is the girl. She has some effect on him.

"Husna, I saw Aroush again today . . ."

Now I get eye contact.

"Outside the base. She was heading toward the mountains. You and your friends come from the mountains, don't you?"

To my relief he speaks. I'm sure it's because I mentioned Aroush. Either that, or the rocket attack has shaken him more than he's letting on. He's a little reluctant, but it's progress. "From south, near Sabz-e Dirang."

At last, confirmation that the Young Martyrs come from the place written on Farshad's photograph. He does not seem overly worried about telling me, probably because finding anything in those mountains would be like trying to find a needle in a haystack.

"All of you?"

"Most, yes. We run away from Taliban." Husna spits angrily. "Farshad go back and find many weapons. He kill guards and we take guns from cave. Now Young Martyrs can fight Americans *and* Taliban."

This is too much to take in. "Hold on, one thing at a time, Husna. The Taliban were after you? Why?"

Husna hangs his head. He's not going to tell me about that one. I wonder if the Young Martyrs have some kind of secrecy-or-death oath.

"Where are the guns, Husna?"

He shrugs again, but he speaks. "Farshad found guns — he didn't show nobody. Don't want Taliban to find cave again so he made explosion to hide entrance."

He can talk about it because he doesn't know the specific location. Great. "Why wouldn't the Taliban just be able to find the place again and open it up?"

"Only two Taliban know where is cave. Farshad hear them

talk and kill them both. Then only he know. Don't tell no one, even Husna don't know."

"If this cave was such a secret, how on earth did Farshad discover it?"

Husna's eyes narrow suspiciously. "Why?"

"Because it's dangerous. Those weapons need to be destroyed. Was Farshad your leader?"

"No. Young Martyrs not need leader. Farshad found guns for us. Many, many guns, that all."

So he had stumbled across that Taliban arms cache high in the mountains and killed the guards.

"How many Young Martyrs are there?"

"Many . . ."

"As many soldiers as there are here?" The garrison is a small affair with about one hundred and fifty soldiers.

He's cagey. "Maybe . . ." is all he will give me.

"And where are your parents?"

No answer to that one.

"You're fighting everybody, aren't you?" I say gently. "The insurgents, us . . . even that Afghan security unit in the village where Farshad died."

Husna won't meet my eyes. He looks away and mumbles, "We want everyone go away. Leave us alone."

"But you're just kids," I remind him, watching his shoulders tense. "Did something happen to your parents?"

There is a painful silence. When Husna turns to face me again, his accusing eyes are bloodshot, holding back tears.

He shouts, "DEAD, ALL DEAD — OK? Happy now? Young Martyrs is Husna's family. The rest is killed by Americans . . . killed by Taliban . . . killed by *you*."

I watch as the boy storms back into his lockup and attempts to slam the door. It shudders to a halt when the bottom catches on a raised patch of earth. Husna rages at it and eventually manages to pull it half shut. Interview over. Now I understand his reaction when he flew at Jackson in McQueen's office. His family was killed and he blames all of us — the Americans most of all.

When I get up to leave, a muffled, sullen voice demands, "When we ever play football?"

It is late by the time I find myself back on my bunk next to Heidi. None of us had wanted to have any time to think about Yugi so, when our shift was over, we all went to the gym — Gizmo, Chip, Jug, and me. That's when I realize what it is there for. It's so that when you feel utterly powerless, when death knocks the stuffing out of you, you can take control of *something*. So you can pound the hell out of a couple of sandbags until you feel like you've fought yourself free from the tangle of grief that holds you. By the time I've finished I don't think I even care about answers or shadows or the Young Martyrs or even Aroush the Afghan girl. I am beginning to doubt everything I've seen. Was it really her I saw walking away from the camp after Yugi died? If so, then every time I have seen her something bad has happened or someone has died, just like Jug said. But he's superstitious and I'm not. There is enough out here to do your head in without adding to it. I can't think about it anymore. All I want now is the oblivion of sleep.

But what I get is Heidi. She's been sitting motionless and in complete darkness on the side of her bunk when I arrive and switch the light on. Her head lifts slightly when I enter and her voice is hollow. "Feel any better?"

I shrug. Like she cares.

There's a long moment of silence. Then she speaks again, but she sounds different now — like it's a real effort to say anything to me. "It just . . . It leaves a hole, that's all. Like your bunk — it was empty for weeks before you got here, and do you know why?"

I shake my head, too tired to talk.

"Because the last medic — Jodie — couldn't take any more stress. She'd had to scrape one too many of her friends off the floor."

Stress? That's a relief. I don't think I could have slept here any longer if she'd died. Not now Heidi has told me her name.

"If you're lucky, you may only have to deal with one. If not, you'll find that when you have more holes than a colander, and everything that you ever were has leaked out, you'll be left with nothing. Like me."

That shocks me. I wonder if she has been drinking, but I know that she's too self-controlled for that, even if there were any out here.

I mutter, "If you're trying to comfort me, it's not working. You don't need to go through this stuff alone and, if you want to stop that colander leaking, why not try opening up a bit? Let someone get close to you for a change."

"What would you know? You don't know me!" Heidi is on her feet, her eyes blazing. Every inch of her body is stretched so tight she could snap.

I hold up my hands. "OK, OK. I'm sorry. Look, you're right — I don't know you. I don't know anything. I'm just tired, really tired."

I'm kicking myself. That was stupid, but I meant well.

The muscles of Heidi's jaw release enough for her to grind out, "For your information, I did 'open up' once. And then I took my eye off the ball and screwed up big-time."

I'm taken aback. "I don't understand. What did you do? What could you possibly have done that's so bad?"

Heidi sits back down on her bunk. There's a long, long silence. "A call came in," she tells me at last, "a male casualty — a rifleman. The idiot had twisted his ankle in a pothole. Not even a combat injury. I was the nearest medic, but I sent the junior medic to deal with it. Toni . . . There was an IED . . ."

She can't bring herself to say what happened, but I can guess. And here I am turning up, acting the hero on my first day. No wonder I got Heidi's hackles up.

"It was fate — that's all. It wasn't your fault. I'm sure you must have had your reasons for sending her," I say.

She grimaces. "Oh yeah, I had my reasons . . . one pathetic reason, if you must know."

"Oh?"

Heidi falls back on her bunk. I can tell that she's closing down. "If you're that desperate to know, why don't you ask Lieutenant Jackson? I'm sure he'd love to fill you in."

Lieutenant Jackson? I don't even know what to think anymore. He's been to this FOB before? Then I remember the way Heidi couldn't look at him, the way she seemed so tired and unhappy when the Americans arrived. They've got some history, then. I don't know why, but my gut twists and I'm upset. Maybe it's because I didn't really need to know that.

"I've seen the way you look at him," Heidi continues, scrutinizing my face for a reaction.

"Look, if you two are an item, that's fine. I'm not interested." I *definitely* don't want to do boy talk like this is some kind of sleepover.

Heidi's voice is flat. "We're not. And the only thing that I care about is my team."

"You could have fooled me."

"I know. For what it's worth, I've been beating myself up about it. Chip's right, I haven't been fair to you."

So that *was* why Chip went to see Heidi that night. He *was* defending me. And here's me thinking those two might be an item. A mixture of gratitude and frustration rattles through me. But he wasn't just thinking about me. I know that. It is the real deal out here — life and death. If Heidi is unprofessional with me, then she plays not just with my life, but the lives of all of us.

"I don't like you," Heidi goes on — *tell me something I don't know* — "and we'll never be friends, but there's no way I am going to put anyone else on my team at risk, even you."

I'm wondering if I should tell her that it's not the best apology I've ever heard, but what she says next silences me.

"One more thing you should know. As Toni left me — I saw the girl, standing on the side of the road. She was giving me this strange, dark look. And I knew she was telling me Toni wouldn't be coming back."

15

THE NEXT DAY IS A REST DAY, AND THERE'S AN almost one hundred percent turnout for the Wainwright Memorial Match. My head is spinning with stuff I can't even begin to think about right now so it's a relief to focus on football — even if I am supposed to be bonding with a homicidal eleven-year-old at the same time. The thought makes me give a wry laugh. No wonder Heidi has lost her marbles — she's been on tour here too often. Husna sticks close to me as we warm up, his eyes wide.

Spectators perch on every available vehicle, sandbag, and oil drum. No trace remains of the craters left by the RPGs. A couple of the lads are even stringing up tarps as sunshades for the spectators. I'm almost past being fazed by anything here — including the fact that we will be playing in what was a battleground and that the Taliban might even be watching the match. It is truly bizarre. The Americans have even managed an impromptu barbecue. I've heard a rumor that Jackson bought a goat from a passing villager. Carlos seems to be in charge of charring bits of it on the smoking grill at the back of his Humvee. He sits there looking pale and flipping burgers with his bayonet.

Heidi emerges from the corridor of blast bags that leads to our bunk room. She's wearing a black T-shirt and has a whistle dangling from a cord round her neck. She's the ref. Fantastic. I might as well pack up and go back to my bunk. When she looks at me, there's not a flicker. No indication that she even remembers our conversation from last night. Bizarre.

All I could find to wear was a pair of cutoff jeans and an old T-shirt. Hardly FA standard, but it'll have to do.

"Everybody ready?" Jackson's come over, holding out a burger to Husna.

The boy refuses to take it.

"It's good!" the lieutenant tells Husna, his eyes flicking toward my cutoff jeans.

"Not before ninety minutes of football in this heat," I say.

There is humor in Jackson's eyes. He looks at me and takes a bite, addressing me and Husna with a lump of half-chewed burger in his cheek. "I guess you're right. Especially when I've got twenty dollars on you scoring two."

My heart sinks as Jackson winks and walks away. I catch sight of Chip on the hood of one of the Hummers. He waves a handful of banknotes at me and grins. He's having the time of his life.

We're playing five-a-side. Husna is up front with me, Gizmo in goal with Greg, and Jug in defense. The field is marked out with wobbly lines drawn in the earth with a stick, and the goals are ingeniously constructed using scaffolding and camouflage nets. Wayne Ritchie looks athletic. He's in his twenties and his face is more suited to rugby than "the beautiful game." Next to him is lanky Phil, a gunner — a good choice of striker if he can hit the ball with his head. But the ones that really make me shudder are their defenders. They are huge — the two of them standing side by side could block the entire goal. All I can hope is that Husna and I can make use of our speed and size to run rings around them. While I'm thinking, my eyes drop from Ritchie's smug face to his foot. It's on the ball. The ball that belonged to Yugi.

Suddenly I don't care about the odds. I just want to win this thing for Yugi. "You take the left wing," I whisper into the boy's ear. "If you get the ball, keep it moving — pass it unless you have a clear shot."

He nods, his warm breath tickling my ear as he whispers back, "Kick arse, Ellie."

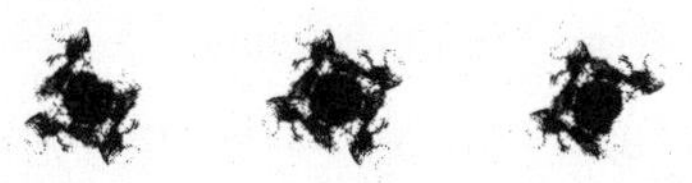

Ritchie is good. He scores one in the first five minutes — after a goal kick flies over Husna's head on the left wing.

Above the cheers and groans I can hear Chip yell, "Where were you, Buffy?" And I remember why I gave up football. It wasn't the game or the prejudice against girls. It was the flipping dads.

Husna glares at our defenders and stamps his foot petulantly, cursing loudly in his own language. The injustice stings me into action. As soon as the whistle blows I kick the ball back to Greg, yelling at him to get it forward. He sends a cracking pass right to Husna, who then takes it neatly between the legs of one of Ritchie's defenders. Ritchie thunders over to tackle the boy, who waits until he's seconds from disaster before ricocheting the ball off Ritchie's calf and right into my path. I weave it round the last floundering defender and knock it past the goalie with a flourish. I'm rewarded with a high five from Husna to a chorus of cheers from the Hummers.

Jackson's on his feet before the net has finished shaking. He's clapping his hands and whooping. "Go, Ellie! You guys see that?"

The celebration is short-lived. They're all over us but can't seem to score, and it's a relief when Heidi blows the halftime whistle. We go another goal down in the second half and everyone is flagging in the heat, especially the big guys. We are all drenched with sweat. All my efforts for our first goal are forgotten. My team is falling apart. Jug and Greg have to be parted by Gizmo because they blame each other when Ritchie gets past me and hits the post. When they are done with each other, they turn on Gizmo. I leave them in disgust and have to waste a couple of valuable minutes trying to get Husna off his backside and back into the match. On the sidelines Chip is arguing with some of the Americans and shooting daggers at me. And all the time Wayne Ritchie is standing at the center line with his foot on Yugi's ball, grinning at our mess.

In the end I get them all around me by our goal. "Grow up, all of you!" I say in exasperation. "Remember who this is for."

They look at me. Even Husna is silenced and he didn't even know Yugi.

"And you're doing this for Farshad," I tell him as an afterthought. I interpret the grunts and backslapping to mean they understand. "Just keep hold of the ball and get it to me or Husna — OK?"

We kick off and keep the ball for all of a minute before they get it back again. How we make it to overtime I'll never know. We're pretty much dead on our feet when, with a spectacular sliding tackle, Jug takes Ritchie down to ecstatic cheers from our supporters. Incredibly, Heidi allows play to continue while he's writhing on the floor, ignoring the screams of *"Foul!"* that are hurled at her from the crowd. Husna gets the ball. It's our last chance to even things up, but both defenders are on him. They back him up to where the sideline used to be before it got trampled out of existence, but Husna manages to lift the ball between them toward me. It curves in a beautiful sweeping arc. I volley it into the back of the net and the roar of the crowd rises around us. Chip runs to hug me and Ben lifts his cap so I can see his sparkling eyes. He's smiling and clapping. Husna falls to his knees with his arms in the air. Then I realize that Heidi is waving her arm. She's blown her whistle and disallowed it. Probably feeling bad about the Ritchie incident.

We're all over her like a rash. Jug's face is red and Gizmo pulls him back to ask, "C'mon Heidi, what was wrong with that?"

"The ball went over the line. It's a throw-in but you'd better be quick. I'm blowing full time fifteen seconds after it's back in play." Heidi throws the ball at Gizmo's chest.

"IS FIX!" Husna yells at the corporal, storming off.

Jug has to follow because he's guarding the boy, and the match ends in total disarray.

I'm left trying to keep the peace between Chip and his punters. He claims that I still got two in the back of the net even if one of them was disallowed.

Thankfully Husna doesn't blame me. When he's over the tantrum, I take him to the shower and make him use it while Jug keeps guard. He's in there for ages, long enough for me to go and wash his clothes. The black stains are definitely blood. They are dry and crusted and turn the water red as I wring the trousers out. When they are as clean as I can get them, I hang them on Heidi's line to dry. She'll hate it. In the meantime Husna seems happy enough to borrow one of my T-shirts and a pair of cargo pants. As I leave to get cleaned up I can't help but smile. The boy is sitting patiently on my bunk next to Jug, sniffing the soft white cotton.

Later Husna and I walk slowly to the empty canteen and find a couple of bottles of water. I wait for him to finish the first, then offer him what's left of mine. He smiles and we sit in companionable silence for a while.

"Was draw," he tells me.

"I know. There's no way you were over the line."

In silent agreement he chugs the last of his water, wiping a few drops that dribble down his chin with his hand.

"Husna?"

He looks at me.

"You know it's time to talk, don't you? Whatever happened to you, whatever made the Young Martyrs so angry, you have to tell someone about it."

Husna is fighting with his emotions. It takes an immense effort for him to keep them under check, and then his face hardens like a mask. I can tell he is forcing himself to speak.

"Something bad is come," he begins, crushing the plastic bottle in his hands and refusing to look at me. "Parents prepare. Tell all of us to run and hide in woods. Farshad find a place. But Aroush will not come! When kids is hide I go back with Farshad and we see what happen. Mother and father still in schoolhouse with Aroush and others . . . All is quiet . . . waiting . . . Far away . . . is noise like humming and flash in sky. Then *Bang! Bang! Bang! BOOM! Bang! BOOM! BOOM!* Fire and smoke everywhere and screaming . . . screaming . . . long time." The boy gasps and drops the bottle, blinking away tears that are flowing freely now. "Some get out from flames and run, RUN! Burning. Some wave at plane — make them stop. Is American — will realize mistake! We go to help but more bomb come, and more! Father is just pieces when I find him, nothing to pick up, nothing! Husna is sick on floor. Can't help it. Everywhere, is more explosion — very close. Then I find Mother — she try to speak with me. I lift her but she scream and wet blood is everywhere — in Husna's hair, in mouth. I cry and cry. Then is quiet again. Except crying and voices coming. Is men — they come to shoot survivor. That when Farshad drag me away. Husna want to stay but can do nothing . . . Husna . . . CAN . . . DO . . . NOTHING."

Husna is breathless with rage, his eyes blank. He collapses onto the table, moaning.

It is a long time before I can venture to put my arm round his shoulder. My whole body is numb. The way he described it, the horrible pallor of his face made it so real. No wonder he hates us — he thinks we did it.

I ask him, "Are you sure they were coalition planes?" It's a daft question. I know that the minute it leaves my lips.

He speaks into his arms, his voice muffled. "We are poor, not stupid."

I grab some paper and a pencil from the kitchen. "Draw them for me."

A shiver runs up my spine as I watch Husna's limp, unwilling hand outline the distinctive angular wings of an unmanned coalition drone bristling with missiles. His heavy strokes almost go through the paper. Helpfully he draws US insignia on the fuselage. Then he holds up three fingers. "This many . . ."

"Can I have this?"

He nods and I fold the picture carefully and put it in my jacket pocket. "What about the men who came?" I can barely bring myself to ask, "Were they in uniform, like us?"

To my relief, he shakes his head.

Now I understand what he said before about the girls from the village. After the bombing Farshad told them to get to safety with his uncle in Pakistan.

I am shocked at what Husna has seen in his short life. Whatever the reality, he believes American planes bombed his family, and there must be many more in these hills who believe the same thing. So much for winning hearts and minds. I draw him to my side, and he doesn't pull away. His head falls against my breast and he cries like a baby, like the lost, lonely boy he is.

Later that day, I find Hammed's chaotic office and convince him that I need to check his wound. I have to find out more about Husna's village and what happened to it and, from what I've been told, what Hammed doesn't know about this part of Helmand isn't worth knowing.

One of Hammed's officers is on his way out when I get there and there's an awkward moment as we both try to pass through the door at the same time. In the end I step back out to let him use it first. Hammed still won't look at me even as I gently remove his *Pakol* and the dressing I put on him yesterday to examine his head. He has a respectable purple lump beneath a bloody knot of gray, wiry hair now, but it is clean and it should heal nicely. So I just tidy it up and re-dress it. While I work on the back of his head I guess that he shouldn't have too much trouble engaging in conversation, since he can't see me anyway. Maybe he can pretend I'm a man.

"The boy I found in Darzab," I begin, "Farshad. Did you know he was from a village near Sabz-e Dirang mountain?"

To my surprise, he answers me. "Yes, yes. Village called Saray. And there is rumor of Western woman coming to live there. Married local man. The woman convert to Islam. They have two children . . ." He stops.

After a moment I fill the gap, "Let me guess, a boy called Farshad and the girl . . . Aroush?"

Hammed just says, *"Allahu Akbar."*

Husna was right, then. Farshad's mum was from the West. Was she a journalist? That would explain the computer Husna saw. But what, I wonder, brought her out here?

16

I'M STILL TRYING TO FIGURE IT OUT AT BREAKFAST the following morning, when Chip informs me that I'm wanted in McQueen's office. Heidi is there, too. She looks away when I approach. Outside, the sun has not even had a chance to lift itself above the horizon. Hammed arrives at the same time as I do. I smile in greeting, but it is wasted because he doesn't even stop to look at me. The warmth of yesterday has vanished. He goes in while I hold up the tarp for him.

"Nielson," the captain greets me as I follow, "how are you getting along with the captive?"

I don't want to say anything about Husna's claim that coalition planes murdered unarmed civilians. I have to know more first. "It's early days, sir. But I think Husna trusts me now — or he's starting to. He told me that Farshad found the arms cache in the mountains. And Hammed knows of his village — it's a place called Saray."

Hammed nods. "Correct. But I do not know where is village, only that is near mountain, Sabz-e Dirang."

"Good work, Nielson. Corporal, your unit is going there with our American friends. You'll report to Lieutenant Jackson."

Heidi flushes. "Sir, may I request another assignment?"

I so need to find out what went on with the lieutenant.

McQueen shuts her up with uncharacteristic firmness, like he's afraid she will embarrass him in front of everyone. "We've already spoken about this, Corporal. Your unit is going with the Americans to try and find the Young Martyrs' arms cache. They — we — want the boy to guide you to his village."

I'll bet they do. Something else is going on here. Navy SEALs reporting direct to General Macallum are not here just to look for a load of guns. But Husna has been through hell and there is no way I'm going to stand by and let him be used. So I swallow my nerves and say, "Sir, with respect, he's just a kid. You're expecting him to act as a reliable guide to a group of people he hates."

"Oh?"

Now I have no choice. I've got to tell him. "Husna thinks coalition planes killed his family."

I pull the picture Husna drew for me out of my pocket and show it to them.

McQueen is as shocked by the picture as I was. "Those look like Predator drones. If it's true — and it's a *big* if — it would have been unintentional. And we can't just take his word for it, Private. He's only a boy."

"I know that, sir, but *he* believes it. He won't want to help us."

The captain raps the desk with his fingers, thinking. "Then we need to find a way to convince him. What if you were to tell him you're going up there to investigate his allegations?"

My jaw tightens so that I can barely squeeze out the words. "But that would be a lie, wouldn't it, sir? And there's another reason the Americans are here, isn't there? I don't think Husna's claims will be high on their agenda."

"The lieutenant may well say more about his mission when he briefs us this afternoon," McQueen tells me flatly. "You'll have to wait until then. In any case, Husna would be more inclined to cooperate if he thinks we can help him — and if the end justifies the means . . ."

I can barely contain myself, though I know I have to. "I thought our brief was to win the hearts and minds of the Afghans, *sir*."

McQueen is beginning to get agitated. "Remember who you are speaking to, Private."

"There's nothing to stop *you* looking into the boy's claims," Heidi puts in.

Very clever. She's giving me the appearance of power. I won't have the authority, the time, or the backup to sidetrack Lieutenant Jackson's mission for one of my own, and she knows it.

"But you know I'm not trained to investigate. I'm a medic."

"Nevertheless" — McQueen gives me a self-satisfied smile, seemingly oblivious to the fact that this is Heidi's play — "you have my permission to investigate Husna's claims if you are able to in the course of your duties. So you *will* tell the boy and get him on our side, understood?"

"Yes, sir." It's an order, then. But I hate it.

To my surprise, Hammed chips in at last. "I will help Private Nielson to do this."

I'm surprised. And grateful, especially when I see the look on Heidi's and McQueen's faces — it's priceless.

McQueen is curt. "You won't be going, Hammed."

"Then how will you negotiate with children?"

The captain grinds his teeth and looks at Heidi. Now that Hammed has a cause, he's going to give them grief.

"Maybe I will go to Kabul and tell Husna's story to newspaper?" Hammed continues. "Afghan people have right to know if coalition planes are killing families. Only way to win war here is with truth — no hiding."

McQueen mouths an expletive and examines the ceiling. "Fine," he says eventually, "go. You're all going, including you,

Corporal — but the boy's allegations are to be taken with a pinch of salt until you have hard evidence. Are we all clear on that?"

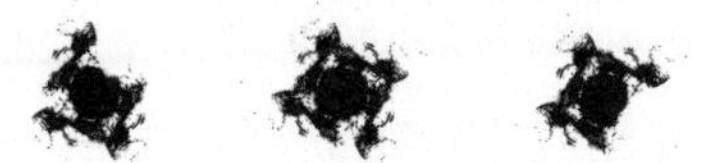

On the way to see Husna I stop off to check on Carlos. I ignore the wolf whistles and crude jokes from his mates when I order him to get his kit off. He's had a restless night, he tells me. The wound kept opening up and has started to weep a clear fluid and his forehead is shiny with sweat. I don't tell him, but I am worried. There's no way he should travel to the mountains with us and the only way it's going to happen is if I improvise something to seal the wound and give his body a chance to start healing. The dressing I put on him yesterday was textbook but my instinct is that he needs something more. Shrapnel wounds have to be sealed to stop dirt getting in. I clean up the entry and exit wounds so well the poor guy looks like he's going to pass out. Then I close the flaps of flesh as neatly and tightly as I can with adhesive stitches. When I'm done, I cover the wounds with my spray-on waterproof dressing and finish it off by wrapping a new dressing round his waist.

My last check is the most important. I need to know if his lungs are going to collapse. "How's your breathing?"

Carlos wipes the sweat from his forehead and gives me a weak smile. "Before you started on me? Fine."

"Good. Any problems breathing, I need to know ASAP."

"Yes, ma'am."

I pack away my kit. "So . . . you guys have been to this FOB before?"

He nods, pulling his shirt back over his head. "We took out a Taliban cell that was giving you Brits some issues."

"I get it. You lot are like the A-Team. You're going to breeze in, fix this mess with a gun battle and a few grenades, and then bugger off into the sunset . . ." There is a scattering of laughter. It dies out when I drop my bombshell. "I don't suppose you know what happened between Lieutenant Jackson and Corporal Larson?"

Carlos smiles. "I can see why Jackson likes you. You don't hold back, do you? That's very Latina. I like you, too. Especially your cold hands. They're the sign of a warm heart."

So, the lieutenant likes me? "What's that, a compliment?"

"Sure . . . he likes people who have opinions and aren't afraid to voice them."

"Well, I . . . respect him. Now, about my question."

"You should ask him yourself. My lips are sealed. I'm Special Forces — you can have my name and rank and that's it!"

There are a few more chuckles at that. But I admire his loyalty. "OK, Sergeant Tough Guy. But I don't think your lieutenant should be playing with your life."

The American drops his voice and inclines his head toward mine. "I trust him with mine and he trusts me with his — that's how it works out here. You should know that. He's a good guy." Then he gets to his feet and flexes his arms. "Nice job!"

I try to ignore the glassy sheen in his eyes.

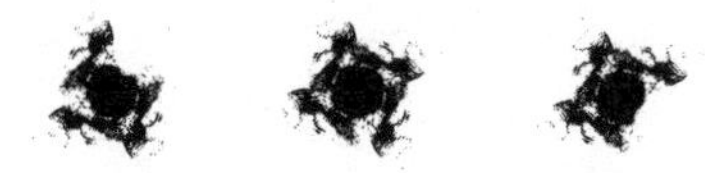

Since his outburst Husna has been going stir-crazy in his little cell. He is pacing by the wall, where he can look out through the slats, a wild creature, used to the great outdoors and to doing whatever he likes. His toy lies on its side in the corner. With his guard's permission I take him outside for some air and let him run off some of his pent-up energy. When he trots back to me, he picks up a rock and dribbles with it. He passes it to me and I place my boot on top of it as it bounces wildly to a halt.

"We play more football?"

"No, Husna . . ." I'm sure he can sense my guilt as I struggle to phrase what I am about to ask him. "Not today." I check the guard is out of earshot.

"What is it?" he demands.

"They want you to guide the Americans to your village."

The boy hacks and spits, and this time I do not comment. He lets off a stream of invective in Pashto and turns a pair of dark, accusing eyes on me. "Husna will rather die," he hisses.

I take him by the shoulders. "You know I talk straight, don't you? No BS."

He hangs his head sullenly.

"Then stop this. Lieutenant Jackson and his guys are not the ones who bombed your village. And guess what? Not all Americans or British or Afghans are bad. In this stupid war — any war — nothing is simple, nothing is black-and-white." I shake him gently. "Do you understand me? The Americans want to know the truth, too." I pause for breath and watch his shoulders sag. Now's the time to play my trump card — and I hate myself for doing it. "Let's work together, Husna. If you help us, I'll investigate . . . I'll try to find out what happened to your family."

"Don't need investigate!" he yells hoarsely, but he's fighting back tears.

I try to stay calm. "Husna, you *do* need an investigation. Someone has to answer for what happened. Someone *will* answer for it. Look at me." I hold his face in my hands and feel a pang of gratitude when he does not pull away. "We're going to Sabz-e Dirang to find the guns Farshad gave you all. But there might be evidence about the bombing, too. We need evidence to get justice for you and your family. To expose the people who did it. I can't promise . . ."

"If I show the Americans, you will do this for me? You will tell world about people who kill?"

I don't hesitate. "Yes, Husna. Yes, I will — somehow. Together we will find a way." I know McQueen didn't mean it, but I do. I really do. I'm determined to help this boy. He has no one in the world to help him. No one except me. He does not need to answer me. When our eyes meet, we have made a pact. The only trouble is, I have no idea how I am going to fulfill my side.

17

THE BRIEFING TAKES PLACE IN THE CLEARED CANteen that afternoon. Husna inhales deeply when we pass through the stale cigarette smoke that lingers by the doorway. Inside, I ignore the raised eyebrows from Chip as Husna and I sit next to him. Captain McQueen and Lieutenant Jackson are already at the front by a whiteboard. Carlos and the rest of the SEALs are lounging in mess chairs. I can feel the tension pull Husna's small frame taut the instant he catches sight of American uniforms. Behind us, Gizmo and Hammed arrive with Heidi. She pushes past me to get to the front with the Afghan, but when she gets there I notice she makes sure that the captain is between her and the lieutenant.

Chip tugs on my sleeve and whispers, “What’s the kid doing here?”

Husna’s eyes flash.

“*The kid’s* name is Husna,” I hiss back at him, “and you can ask him yourself.”

“Well?” Chip asks Husna, but the boy just gives him a dirty look. Chip tilts his head at me. “So . . . I asked . . .”

“He’s going to help us find his village.”

Chip looks horrified. “Are they nuts? You know we’re just going along as cannon fodder, don’t you? And you can bet that Ronald McDonald up there is going to have all the fun while we have to babysit the Kamikaze Kid here. With him leading us we might as well have *Shoot Me, Raghead* tattooed on our foreheads.”

“Do you have to use that word in front of him?”

He laughs. “I hardly think he needs protecting, Buffy.”

Husna butts in before I have a chance to open my mouth. “I not Kamikaze Kid. Am man of honor and Ellie is my friend.”

“Excuse my skepticism, but I’ve seen your lot at work,” Chip retorts as he turns back to watch the lieutenant take the floor. “They change sides more often than a bloody tennis ball.”

I shush him. Jackson has taped a map to the whiteboard and turns to wait for silence. That’s all he needs to do, turn and wait. Everyone’s eyes fix on him.

"OK. Now that we're all here, let's cut to the chase. Our intel tells us that Taliban insurgents have been stockpiling arms somewhere in the mountains. We think they've been using this route to smuggle arms in via Pakistan." Jackson waves his red laser pointer in a wobbly circle around Sabz-e Dirang mountain on the wall map. His shirtsleeve falls back to reveal the tattoo I saw when the Americans drove in. Now I can see that it's a faded crown of thorns snaking around his right bicep. It's really nice work, too — tasteful, understated. I try not to fixate on the way it moves as he points and then I realize that he is still speaking.

". . . somehow these weapons have found their way into the hands of a group of kids calling themselves the Young Martyrs. We have no idea, as yet, what has happened to their parents."

Husna swears loudly in English and wins a respectful glance from Chip. "Is lies, American lies. They know."

Jackson continues smoothly. "So we're tasked with finding the arms cache, closing the arms route, and disarming the children." Jackson's eyes flick at me and I realize he's reading me. He suspects that I know there's more to his mission than he's letting on. "Any questions?"

I look around the room. Heidi is leaning against the wall by the whiteboard, not even looking at it. Her arms are folded firmly across her chest and her eyes are shooting daggers at Jackson's back.

Chip's hand shoots up. "What if the kids resist? They're pretty handy with those weapons. You want us to engage minors, Lieutenant?" His face is gray with the memory of his last kill.

McQueen grimaces. He chews at his bottom lip, embarrassed by Chip's blunt question.

Jackson looks him in the eye and I find myself admiring the direct way he deals with everything. When Heidi turns my way, I try not to look at her. "It's Chip, isn't it? Truth be told, Chip, I'm hoping Husna here will negotiate with them . . ."

I feel the Afghan boy tense, but to my relief he stays quiet.

When he has waited to see if there will be any more questions, Jackson pulls down the map. "If nobody else has anything we'll get on to the other reason we need to take a look around Sabz-e Dirang. You've all been carefully selected to be here and you should know that what you are going to see and hear is classified. It goes no farther than this room."

I knew it. Finally we're going to find out what's really going on.

With a wave of his hand to one of his guys, Jackson stands to one side and an image is projected onto the whiteboard.

It is a grainy picture of the Afghan girl in the blue dress, taken at some distance through clouds of dust with a high-powered lens.

I open my mouth to speak, but Heidi's eyes flash at me and she says quickly, "That's the girl Nielson and I saw at the IED."

"She's from Husna's village. You've known her for a long time, haven't you, Husna?"

He's not ready to give anything to the Americans yet, and just looks at the floor with his arms folded tightly across his chest.

Jackson's looking at me for a reaction when he says, "We've had reports of sightings in this area. Our instructions are to locate her, if she is still alive, and return her *safely* to HQ in Kabul . . ."

Now Husna breaks his silence. He looks at me like I have betrayed him. "Aroush will never do this!"

Jackson shakes his head patiently. "She has family, in America, Husna. Someone who loves her and wants her back."

Husna looks sullen. "Aroush belong here."

Hammed adds pointedly, "Girl is Afghan."

Now Jackson tells the others what I've already heard from Husna. "That's not completely true, Hammed. As I'm sure you know, she has dual nationality. Her mother was an American." Then, with a deep breath, as if deciding whether or not to share the information, he adds something more, "And she wasn't just *any* American."

"Make no difference," says Hammed.

Husna is nodding and frowning at the same time.

Jackson continues. "But it's her mother's *name* that is important. Bella *Macallum*." Murmurs begin to fly around the room. "I can see the name is familiar to everyone here, with the possible exception of Husna." He looks confused until Jackson says, "This little Afghan girl is the granddaughter of the commander of US forces in Afghanistan, General John Macallum."

"NO!" It's Husna and he's looking at me, processing the information. "Mother of Aroush is just from West."

"That's all you would have been told, Husna," Jackson tells him gently. "She wouldn't have wanted anyone other than her husband to know she was related to an American general."

No wonder they want to find Aroush. No wonder they've sent SEALs. And to think I've been nearly close enough to touch her.

Into the silence that eventually falls, I say, "In that case, Lieutenant, you'd better tell the general that she is still alive. I saw her after the RPG attack. But he should know that his grandson is dead."

18

THE LIEUTENANT TAKES HIS CAP OFF AND RUNS his hands through his hair, putting it back on afterward. It seems to be his trademark thinking gesture. "A grandson?" he asks me. "Are you sure?"

It's the first time I've seen Jackson rattled. I'd enjoy it if he didn't seem quite so stressed by what I've said. The whole room has noticed. I feel for him. He wraps the briefing up quickly, telling us to be ready to leave for the mountains in one hour, then ushers me and Husna into the mess kitchen, closing the door behind him. He leans against the wall next to Husna, sandwiching him between us, so that he has to speak to me over the boy's head.

"So what's this about the girl having a brother?" he demands. "And why didn't you mention it before?"

I drop my eyes, embarrassed. There wasn't time, it didn't seem important, and if I'm honest, I wasn't sure I could trust him. He notices my awkwardness and, to my relief, doesn't press me. He's obviously guessed why. I look up again.

"I'm sorry, Lieutenant. The boy Chip and I found, Farshad, was about sixteen. We never told anyone — but the girl was there, too. I've seen her two other times."

"Did you at least go to McQueen with any of this? What makes you think they were related?"

I don't know what to say. The way he asks makes me think I was stupid not to say anything. I must look like a complete idiot to him.

"I tell Ellie," Husna butts in.

Jackson shakes his head. "This doesn't make any sense. Why didn't Macallum tell *me* about the boy? Surely he'd want us to locate him, too."

"Is true," Husna looks at me and his eyes ask the question *Are they all this dim?* "Farshad was brother of Aroush. Live in same village as me."

"Maybe the general thinks that Farshad is somewhere safe," I say, "out of harm's way."

The lieutenant frowns, his eyes wrinkling while he thinks. He's not convinced. "Maybe."

"Why did the general's daughter decide to leave the States to live out here?" I ask.

"She worked for the *Washington Post* covering Middle Eastern politics. That's all I know, other than while she was out here she fell in love. Take it from me, her father didn't approve of the match."

"You know that Aroush isn't going to be in the area around Sabz-e Dirang?" I ask Jackson.

He shakes his head. "I think she will."

"No, really, she's here somewhere."

"She might have been, but the Young Martyrs are based in the mountains, aren't they, Husna?"

Husna won't look at either of us.

The American laughs. "Thought so. And after their recent action around here, I'll bet they're heading back there to regroup. And where the Young Martyrs go, so will Aroush."

"Farshad had a family photograph, taken in the mountains," I say.

"Do you have it?"

He does not seem surprised when I say, "No."

"Would you recognize the place if you saw it?"

I don't know, but I remember the distinctive jagged peak behind the whitewashed house. Husna shuffles his feet. I think he knows that the American is hedging his bets, just in case our guide has any intention of leading us astray.

After the briefing Husna comes with me to help me pack my gear, then we head back out to the compound. The muted hum of conversation fills the air. Jackson asks Chip, Gizmo, and me to follow him with Husna and leads us toward the first idling Humvee.

The squat beige vehicles, their awkward-looking M2 guns perched on top like an afterthought, are already rattling away like old washing machines. They look primitive alongside our two heavily armored, caterpillar-tracked Warthogs, which pull up behind them in a swirl of dust and grit.

"Jeez," Chip mutters, "haven't you lot heard of IEDs?"

Jackson laughs. "We like to feel the wind in our hair — to be at one with the road."

I know what he means. I've only been here a few days but I understand now that most of the guys think the MRAPs are useless. When they are not immobilized by IEDs, they are always breaking down. Perhaps sometimes it's better to take the risk in a vehicle that can at least get you to your destination.

Chip shakes his head in mock disbelief, but I can tell he likes the American. "If we roll over an IED, you'll be at one with the road all right — and at one with the Humvee, the bushes, some insurgent with a detonator . . ."

None of us laughs.

We follow Lieutenant Jackson to the first in the line of dusty, dented vehicles and clamber inside. Carlos, his forehead beaded with sweat, and a couple of other Navy SEALs sit grim-faced on the opposite bench as we duck our heads and enter. Looking at the flimsy armored panels, I try not to think how much safer we would be with the rest of our lads.

The Humvee jerks forward and we all lurch with it as it accelerates out of the compound, followed by the other and then the Warthogs, barely visible behind us in the dust storm we kick up. Carlos winces at the violent movement and turns his face from me. Through the mud-smeared rear window I watch the gates of the base close behind us. A few seconds later we are passing through the old olive grove and heading toward the mountains. Did I really see Aroush walking this way after Yugi died? Or was it just a trick of the light, something to do with the stress? As we leave the grove behind I imagine her light, bare footprints being crushed beneath our lurching tires.

19

FOR FOUR HOURS WE TRAVEL DEEPER INTO ENEMY territory. Anywhere else the journey would only take two, but we have to make constant stops to check for IEDs and possible ambush points. For the first hour, every time our vehicle lurches to a halt nerves cramp the pit of my stomach and I find myself waiting for the inevitable. At least it's not a helicopter. Judging by the pale, serious faces opposite me I'm not the only one who has images of those wrecked MRAPs at the base flashing through my head. It helps to watch Husna, who is leaning against me with a bemused smile stretched across his face. He must be pleased not to be walking all the way, as he will have done many times.

Soon, though, even Husna stops smiling, and I wonder when he's going to ask me if we're nearly there yet. He never does. Kids out here know how to wait. Watching those big brown eyes I struggle to imagine how he'll ever come to terms with what he's been through. And that makes me think of Jackson, seemingly so at ease with himself and his unreal life. How does he do it? Everyone knows that Special Forces training is enough to scar most people for life — let alone some of the missions they have to go on.

We climb higher into the foothills and the road gets more and more potholed and each time the Hummer drops into a deep crater I find myself lifted from my bench in a moment of heart-stopping weightlessness. It's a relief when the first part of the journey is finally over and I can jump out of the back door and gaze at the towering, gray mountain of Sabz-e Dirang.

We set up camp in the shadow of the mountain, before the sun drops behind it and leaves us wrapped in the cool, forbidding Afghan night. A line of lower peaks rises above us, ancient and weary like a bunch of bent old men, their heads topped with wisps of white cloud.

We are deep in Taliban territory now and it is hard not to imagine that there are insurgents everywhere, just waiting for an opportunity to send us to our graves. We set up a perimeter formed by our vehicles and a wall of higher ground, and everyone goes about their tasks without speaking. At least our sand-colored army tents go up quickly. Nothing like the things my dad used to wrestle with on family camping trips.

The canvas of my tent ripples in the light breeze, and I worry about how thin and flimsy it is. It's too easy to forget where you are when you pull the zipper and shut out the world. Memories of the RPG attack flood back and I have to busy myself to banish the image of Yugi lying in a pool of his own blood.

Out here we can't risk using lights for anything. I have night-vision goggles as part of my kit, but because they run on batteries I'm keeping them for combat only. Just as a precaution I test them, and watch Heidi and Gizmo helping Hammed with his tent in a painfully bright, luminous green world. I've only ever used them a couple of times before, in a training exercise, and it takes me a while to find the dimmer. When the moon is up there is plenty of light anyway, once your eyes get used to it. It's going to be even colder here at night than at Freeman. I can feel icy air dropping from the high ground and wrapping itself around me as if it can't wait to leech away all the heat of the day. I shiver and locate Jackson. He's at the Hummer, rummaging in his backpack. He pulls out a crumpled, crackling red packet and throws it to Husna.

"Here! My last one, so eat 'em where I can't see you," he jokes.

Husna is caught unawares. His reflex is to catch the gift. He stands with his arms half raised as the pack hits his chest and falls to the ground with a rattle.

I pick it up for him. It's a packet of M&M'S, peanut butter flavor. "You'll never make the cricket team," I joke while I open it for him and wait for his fist to unclench, knowing he'll find it too hard to resist a sugar rush. At last he opens his fingers and I pour some candy onto his palm. Husna crunches away uncertainly at first. Then he takes the packet from me with a greedy glint in his eye.

"Hey — share them around!" I say hopelessly to his back. "And you might like to thank the lieutenant!"

It's not going to happen. He's off to find somewhere private.

I shrug and turn to see Jackson watching me as he directs his SEALs to set up defensive positions. I find myself battling a rushing sound that rises in my ears. My heart is racing — what is that about? I seriously need to get a grip. Checking my kit seems like the thing to do, even though I've already been through it twice. You never know.

The wind strokes my face while I work. It's not much, but it's enough to make the pine trees in the valley below us hiss and shake. Up here the hard mountain walls funnel it into moaning swirls of dust that coat everything with a matte gray layer and exhaust themselves almost as fast as they rise. Beneath one of the Hummers a lone rust-brown sparrow plays in a pool of moonlight, flicking dirt onto its back in a feathery blur. It's cute. Reminds me of home.

Heidi tells us to guy our tents to the vehicles in case the breeze turns into something more serious. To my relief, she has decided that sharing with me and Husna is beyond the call of duty, so she's pitched her tent with Chip and Gizmo. I note that it's about as far away from the Americans as she can get. When Husna has finished his sugary feast he helps me in companionable silence. By the time we've had something to eat, he looks done in. It makes me realize how young he is. I let him curl up in the sleeping bag I found for him at the base and just sit there watching him for a while. As his breathing slows and the cool mountain air seeps into my bones the tent zipper hums. I jump a mile.

The flap flutters open. It's Carlos. "Elinor!" His voice drops to a whisper when he notices that Husna is sleeping. "The lieutenant wants to see you."

Now what? I scramble out, and bump into Heidi.

"How's the injury, Sergeant?" she inquires.

"Awesome, thanks to Private Nielson." But we both heard Carlos gasp as he stood up. He waits to one side for me to join him.

"I checked his wound this morning," Heidi informs me.

"And?" I wait for the criticism.

She's quiet for a second. "It's nice work. But don't get complacent. We need to keep an eye on him."

I'm shocked. Why is she being nice? What is she after? "Oh, OK. You think he still needs evacuating?"

She shrugs. "Maybe. But you seem to have prevented any infection. Well done."

I'm still dumbfounded. "Thanks . . ."

Heidi turns her back on me. "Keep your thanks. When a member of my team does well, I let them know. That's all."

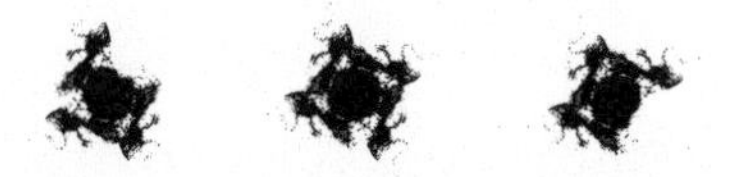

Lieutenant Jackson is sitting on a box of ammo in a secluded spot by the front wheel of one of the Hummers. Carlos throws him a greeting, then leaves us alone. The lieutenant has the satellite phone in one hand and a map in the other. He is wearing a khaki T-shirt under his open jacket. My eyes drift to the silver dog tag next to the dent in his neck. When I look up, I realize he's staring right at me. I blush bright red, caught in the act. What am I doing? It's even worse that I can't seem to control it. Thank God it's dark. He indicates the box beside him and shifts to the edge so that I can sit down at his side. Our thighs touch for a moment, and he frowns and moves to increase the space.

He begins to talk without looking at me. "I've got to speak to Macallum and I might need to put you on."

"The commander, sir?"

"You can lose the 'sir' for tonight, Ellie." To my surprise there's doubt in his blue eyes when he looks at me, as well as something else I can't quite read. But I love the way he says my name. Like it's the most natural thing in the world, like we're friends. "I need your help. He's sent us out here without all the facts and I'm not about to risk any lives without knowing why. If he's holding something back, I need to know that he at least has a good reason. Maybe what you say will draw him out. I'd like you to tell him about his grandson, how he died." His voice seems weighed down by responsibility.

He is only twenty-three and yet he's leading us all into the unknown.

For a moment his words have put me back in that room, kneeling over Farshad with the photo of his family lying next to his heart, and all my senses are raw with the waste of that young life. Aroush, his sister, has lost everyone who ever meant anything to her and seems to be just wandering aimlessly around Helmand, getting herself shot. Getting herself shot? She wasn't even scratched. I can't begin to think how I could have imagined something so violent, so real. But I was in the middle of a gunfight — maybe stress can do that to you. Still, I could swear I'd been looking right at her, eye to eye — and the same eyes told me there wasn't a mark on her. I shake the thought out of my head and consider something else — if Aroush's mother, Bella Macallum, was here against her father's wishes, hiding her identity, does the girl even know who her grandfather is?

"I still wonder how Macallum's daughter ended up staying in Afghanistan," I say slowly. "If she'd lived in a big town like Kabul, I could understand, but out here?"

Jackson turns the phone over in his hand. "All I know is his daughter was on a long-term assignment for her paper. She ended up living with some Afghan guy. They obviously found love — the real thing. They say it makes you foolish, right? Not that I'd know. Being a SEAL is all I've ever wanted to do."

"There must have been . . . I mean a guy like you . . ." I stop myself.

"No one that really mattered." He turns the phone over in his hands. "When I say the SEALs have been my life, I mean it. But after four tours out here it makes you think, you know . . ."

I do know.

". . . that there should be more. That you should do more before your time is up."

The mention of his previous tours triggers something in my memory. Like an idiot, I blurt, "So what happened with you and Heidi?"

Jackson's eyebrows arch. "Me and who? The corporal?"

I want to curl up and die. But it's out now and there's no going back.

"You're something else, you know that?" He's looking at me strangely. "Nothing happened between us. I just met her before, that's all. We'd taken out a Taliban cell. One of their top guys was badly injured, but we needed him alive so we carried him back to the FOB. As I remember, it was called FOB Resolute back then. I asked this medic there — Toni Freeman — to take care of him. Your corporal said Freeman was needed elsewhere and did the work herself. She was crazy good, saved his life. Next I know, we heard that Freeman had been killed. She stepped on an IED. I'm no shrink, but I think your corporal blames herself."

Now I wish I hadn't asked. And he's still looking at me, trying to work it out.

"Why did you want to know?"

"I'm new. She's been acting strangely since I arrived and all I could get out of her was that it was something to do with you."

He picks up his cap and brushes the dust off it. I wonder if I've overstepped the mark.

"I'm not good at reading the signs," he says slowly, "but I get the feeling . . . you know. That she may have a thing for me."

"It's not hard . . . I mean to *see* she has a thing for you . . . not to *have* a thing for you . . . to see that someone *might* . . ." I want to curl up and die again.

To my relief, he ignores my embarrassment and picks up his thread. "Man, I hope not. But I've never encouraged her. The opposite, in fact."

He looks troubled now and it just confirms that I am officially an idiot. I should have left well enough alone. "Forget I asked. It's me — curiosity runs in the family. It ruins surprises — birthdays, Christmases, the lot — believe me."

I'm rewarded with a wry smile. "How did we even get on to this?"

"Bella Macallum. You said she fell in love with an Afghan."

"Yeah, right. Macallum hit the roof when he found out, told her to leave the guy, but she wouldn't hear of it. A couple of months later she was married and expecting a baby. She wrote a letter once telling him not to look for her, that she was happy, but the general didn't buy it. He thinks she was forced to convert to Islam by her husband and kept here against her will. In the end she cut all ties with him."

I think of her laughing face in Farshad's photo. It was not the face of a kidnapped woman.

"I don't know for sure, but I think he pulled some strings with the CIA and traced her to south Afghanistan." He waves the phone at the towering black rocks. "Somewhere in the foothills of Sabz-e Dirang to be precise."

"To Saray — Husna's village?"

He shakes his head. "Macallum didn't know the exact location, just the area. He was about to go looking for her, but 9/11 happened and the War on Terror got in the way. Sightings of the girl, Aroush, must have given him some hope of at least locating his granddaughter. Now that he's finally here in Afghanistan and in charge, he's trying to do just that."

"You don't think the arms cache is an excuse, that he's just sending us out here to look for her, do you?"

He hesitates, unwilling to speak against a superior officer. In the end all he says is "His judgment may be clouded because she's family. But, no, I don't think Aroush or the arms cache are the only reasons we're here. There's something else. Something to do with Bella and what else she was doing in Afghanistan. I think she sniffed out a big news story."

"But you can't blame him for wanting to find his granddaughter."

"Even so, the general should have told me Aroush had a brother. Out here, having the full information can mean the difference between living and dying."

Jackson punches the buttons on his phone and puts it on speaker. In the still of the night I hear the phone ringing, then a tinny voice answers curtly, "Macallum."

It puts the fear of God in me. To us foot soldiers, Macallum is God.

"Sir, it's Ben Jackson."

"You found her?"

"No, sir, we haven't, but something has come up."

The voice turns cautious. "Oh?"

Jackson takes the bull by the horns. "Sir, you didn't tell me that you also had a grandson."

The line falls silent, then the voice spits out, "Had?" The guy doesn't miss a thing. "I don't. What happened?"

"Sir, Aroush's brother was killed in a gun battle a few days ago."

Silence.

"Sir?"

When he speaks again, Macallum's voice sounds tired. "Jackson, you're there to do a job, just do it. I'm sorry the kid's dead, but Bella's husband had already fathered a boy. The kid is . . . was Aroush's half brother. He's irrelevant — I didn't know him. All I want to know is what happened to my daughter and if my granddaughter is still alive. Bella's dead — she would have found some way to reach me by now if she wasn't. But Aroush is still out there. I know it."

"With respect, sir, is there something more I need to know?"

"I've told you what I want."

Jackson's tone is serious. "Yes, sir. But if I'm to risk my men's lives I need to have all the facts. And there's something else you need to hear — a young boy the Brits captured says he is part of a gang called the Young Martyrs, claims that Predator drones were in action in the mountains around Sabz-e Dirang. He says that civilians in Saray were deliberately targeted . . . ."

So McQueen told him Husna's story. I don't know whether to feel grateful or angry. Will the lieutenant help Husna, or try to bury the evidence?

Again the response is a long time coming.

"Sir?" Jackson looks at the phone. "Sir, are you still there?"

He is just about to press the "end call" button when the earpiece crackles. Macallum speaks with irate precision. "Let me make this crystal clear. The US Army does not target civilians, Lieutenant. All I know is something happened on that mountain, and whatever it was affected my family. I want you to find out what happened to Bella — and Aroush is the key. So follow your *orders* and keep your eyes open. That is all. Now I don't want to hear from you again until you have specific news about the operation for me."

Before Jackson has time to respond the phone clicks and the line goes dead. "I guess he doesn't think a step-grandson he never met counts for much," he says. "You're off the hook."

The sudden realization that I don't want to be off the hook, that I want to prolong this moment, is a shock. Now I understand Heidi, why she wanted to be close to him. There's something about him . . . the way he speaks, the way he always seems so self-assured.

When I don't move, Jackson makes no attempt to dismiss me. Instead he pulls out a battered iPod, pushes one earbud into his ear, and clambers up onto the roof of his Humvee. "What kind of music are you into?" he asks me, holding out his hand.

For a moment I'm not sure what to do. He's a superior officer. Back home I could convince myself that we were off duty, but here? There is no *off duty*. I can see he's beginning to wonder why the hesitation, so I ditch the thinking thing, take his hand, and scramble up.

"Anything, I guess, pop punk, *some* dubstep, and rock. I like rock."

"Old or new? I've got AC/DC, the Stones, Zeppelin, Aerosmith . . ."

"New! The Strokes, Muse, Yeah Yeah Yeahs, and that sort of thing. I can't take Aerosmith seriously since Steven Tyler did *American Idol*."

He laughs. "At least he was fair."

"And Cowell was honest. I like honesty."

"Me too. And . . . I like people who care." He gazes at me when he says it, and for a moment — the smallest moment — I can't tear my eyes from his. Then he looks down, handing me the other earbud and tapping the "play" button.

He sits and I have to follow suit so I can put the earphone in, and we stay there, gazing up at the sky while a jangling guitar riff melts into the thumping drum and bass. I can feel the gap between my arm and his like it is something solid. The iPod wire dangles between us and I watch it sway gently for a moment, enjoying the music in one ear and the soft night sounds in the other. Somewhere in the distance an owl hoots. When I look above my head there must be a billion stars up there. I'm lost for words. It's so beautiful.

"It's not often you get to listen to great music under a sky like this," Jackson says, leaning back on his elbows.

He's right. Back home only the brightest stars have the strength to outshine our light pollution. Here the sky is better than any work of art. It is the blackest of blacks and the Milky Way is an arcing band of light. It is enough to take your breath away, to make you forget everything, to lose yourself.

Chris Martin starts singing "Yellow." He tells us to look at the stars. They're shining for me, apparently. I give Jackson a reproachful look.

"Don't flatter yourself," he says, and we both laugh.

"Yes, sir . . . but Coldplay?"

He grins, and his eyes glint with reflected light. "I told you, lose the 'sir.' Call me Ben."

"Ben . . ."

I like it. I like the way he watches my lips as I say it. He clears his throat and turns away.

It's like a splash of cold water. The sudden realization that we are here and this is wrong. And now I'm scared. More scared than I have been since I first set foot in Helmand. I'm scared that this is the start of something that could wound me as badly as any bullet. Suddenly I'm remembering Heidi's pain. I give him back his earbud and slide off the roof.

"I should go," I tell him as I drop to the ground. All the time I can feel his eyes on my neck. When I turn around, I can barely bring myself to catch his eye. The way he looks at me makes me feel like I'm being so stupid.

"Hey, if you have to go, you have to go," he says good-naturedly, popping my earbud in and folding his arms behind his head. "But you're going to miss the best show on earth."

I laugh as I walk away, but I'm trying not to feel hurt by the matter-of-fact way he said it, as if he doesn't care if I stay or go. I hope he's just covering up how he feels. Then I could let myself believe that he's scared, too, and that we're thinking exactly the same thoughts.

20

WE BREAK CAMP JUST BEFORE DAWN. OUR GEAR is wet with mountain dew. The day is warming up enough to start the crickets chirping again and I think that might mean it's going to be a hot one. But there is a crispness to the air that is totally different to the dry, still atmosphere that smothers FOB Freeman. If you close your eyes and forget that you are in a war zone, it's so nice up here. And there is something about having Husna with me that reminds me of my brother and adds to my confusion. I catch Jackson — Ben — watching me when I'm rolling up the tent, but he looks away when our eyes meet. He's outlining his plans to Carlos, professional again, like I should be.

Heidi is waiting impatiently for me with Chip, Gizmo, and the others. I've been taking too long because I let Husna think he was helping. She looks stressed already and I wonder what she really feels for Ben now. From where I'm standing the passing of time doesn't seem to be helping her at all. She's certainly keeping her distance.

For some time we continue climbing higher and higher into the mountains, past a sheer rock face and through several mountain passes. Being in the Hummer is as physical as walking, and it lurches like it's on legs, not wheels. The road has been bad up till now, but it is becoming impassable. The guys on the guns scan the high places and dense scrub for any signs of movement while the roar of our engines echoes around and the dust our vehicles raise hangs in the air behind us. Everyone within twenty miles must know we're here. When we finally lose sight of the plains behind us, Chip taps my arm.

"Congratulations, Buffy," he says, grinning, "your first tour on the front line and already you've gone farther than any coalition forces have ever been."

He's not helping my nerves. I'm wondering how long we'll have to wait if we need help.

After another hour or so we reach the end of our journey. It's a high spot with good natural defenses — a kind of dip in the ground just off the road, surrounded with large boulders where we can remain hidden. I can almost hear everyone sigh with relief when the engines fall silent.

From here we can see a good ten miles into the river valley beyond. Sabz-e Dirang mountain is close now, rising up over the lowland opposite. And the sound of the river is loud even from this distance. Its banks are thick with vegetation, some of it set out in neat, geometrical shapes, clearly planted by human hands. In places I can see glimmering braids of water between the greenery, winding into the distance until the river is hidden completely by a dense pine forest at the head of the valley.

We all get out of our vehicles and Ben addresses us on the move. It's a while before I realize why he doesn't just call us all together — if we're being watched no one will suss that he's our leader. I can't tell if he's feeling awkward about last night or whether he's just not making eye contact with me because he's in professional mode. Maybe all that stuff on top of the Hummer was nothing more than he made it seem. I'm so confused. Stuff that; I'm an idiot. This isn't the place for me to lose my grip on reality. It's Afghanistan, for God's sake, and we are deep in enemy territory. I'm a soldier and I have a job to do and I'm not going to let anything get in the way. A glance in Heidi's direction helps me to firm up my resolution.

"We'll be going the rest of the way on foot and off-road," Ben tells us.

All the Navy SEALs and half of my unit — me, Husna, Heidi, Chip, and Gizmo — are to go on the expedition, while the other half — including Jug — are to stay to protect the vehicles and cover our backs.

Then he adds, "If all goes well, we should return here in two days."

I go to check on Carlos while everybody is getting their kit together. He's sitting on a rock with his head in his hands and he doesn't move when I squat at his side.

"Let me look."

He raises his arm without speaking and I lift his jacket and tug his T-shirt away from the bandage. Underneath, the wound is an angry red. Despite the pain he's in, it actually looks like it might be on the mend. But his general condition worries me. "I need to speak to Ben," I mutter, starting to get up, but Carlos grabs my arm and looks at me with iron determination on his face.

"The doc gave you injections for me, right?"

I nod. "They're in my pack."

"Let's do it, then. Once I've had my shots, I'll be fine."

All this machismo is starting to get to me, and I almost give him the privilege of hearing my unbiased opinion on the matter, but I sense soldiers like this have to be at death's door before they even concede they need help.

I sigh. "OK, but here's the deal — if you get any worse afterward, I'm calling in the Black Hawks whether you want me to or not."

"Deal," he hisses through gritted teeth.

I don't let him see that my hands are shaking when he

lowers his trousers for me to jab the syringes into the top of his backside.

Ten minutes later, as we wait to leave the safety of our vehicles, I ask Gizmo and Chip to help me keep an eye on Carlos. They seem unconcerned. It is almost like it is an affront to their collective male pride that I have even asked.

Chip's response is gruff. "He looks fine to me."

And Gizmo just mumbles, "If he's stupid enough to carry on with a shrapnel wound, that's up to him."

But I know they will both watch him like hawks.

Ben comes over to us before we set off. "This is it, then," he tells us. "We'll descend into the valley using the forest down there for cover until we reach the river. From here to the trees, keep to goat or rabbit tracks — anything with fresh droppings — if it's safe for them it should be OK for us. When we get to the valley floor, we'll take another look at the best way to go. Oh, and Husna" — he smiles at the boy — "we're going to need you later to show us the best route into Saray."

Husna looks away. "Nothing in Saray now."

"We'll see. Think you can find it from here?"

The boy looks like he's been given a lemon to suck. He's insulted. "Could find it from other side of Afghanistan." But he looks at me as if to remind me of my promise. He'll only be our guide if I find out about the bombing of his village.

Ben snorts. "That's what I was hoping. You can stay up front with me and Ellie here." His hand seems to rest on my arm slightly longer than it should.

Suddenly I'm aware that Chip and Gizmo are watching us from the other side of the camp. Worse, some of the Americans are looking, too. My gun slips in my grip with a noisy rattle and I hold it tighter, hoping they don't connect my clumsiness with how self-conscious I must look. The last thing I want is to make anything difficult for Ben. To my major embarrassment, though, my cheeks flush again and I have to turn and hide my face. It's ridiculous. I've got to find some way to control this.

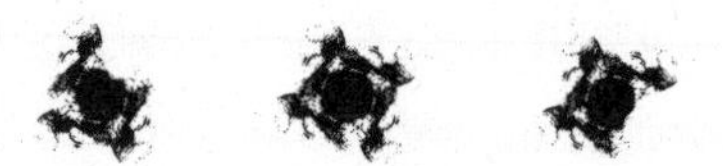

We set off down the valley, marching warily over the bleak, boulder-strewn mountainside. Husna stays close to me all the time, eyeing our guns. I wonder what he'd do if he managed to grab one. The gravel crunches beneath our feet as we march and above our heads dark clouds gather. This is so different from previous patrols in the lowlands where we would meet people all the time. Here everything is silent and heavy with expectation. The hairs on the back of my neck are dancing. While we are in the open and overlooked by so many rocky hiding places it's hard not to imagine Taliban crosshairs trained on your head. Adrenaline spreads like fingers of ice through my chest, and I have to breathe deep and long just to calm down. Out here it could all be over before air support even gets a visual on us. And it would take hours for McQueen to get any reinforcements this deep into enemy territory.

Ben walks ahead of me, in control. I take some comfort from it. Then, realizing where my thoughts are going, I force myself to look away and put him totally out of my mind. Humidity seems to squeeze all the oxygen from the air around us and makes our breathing labored as we descend the steep valley sides. Stones rattle and skit around us like tiny avalanches. Sweat trickles in cool lines over my ribs and soaks into the belt of my trousers.

As we walk I wonder what happened to Bella Macallum. Is she really dead? The general seems to think so. Her daughter is running wild and her stepson is dead. Unless she's a terrible mother — which, somehow, I doubt — something bad *has* happened to her. And that has to be one of two things — she's dead or a captive. If she was a captive they'd probably be trying to get a big ransom from her paper or the Americans, and it would be international news. So Macallum must be right. Perhaps she was killed in the bombing Husna witnessed. But he never mentioned her. That photograph with her last message to them scrawled on the back makes me think she knew something bad was going to happen. From what Husna told me the villagers were expecting something — that's why they sent the kids away.

I grip my rifle tightly and scan the slopes as we approach the lush, green pine forest beneath us. A couple of Ben's men stop every now and then to scan the dense undergrowth with heavy thermal-imaging devices. The equipment the SEALs have is unreal. Our guys cast envious looks their way. Me, I'm just happy they're on our side. I remember stories I've heard of Afghan snipers sitting high in the trees for cover and spraying automatic fire on patrolling troops. It is a relief when the SEALs lower their scopes and wave the all clear.

On my left, Chip's shoulders are taut, his gun is raised, and his finger coiled around the trigger ready to pull. I copy his stance. When we enter the trees the tension rises — there are no clear paths or animal tracks. We have to thread our way through the trunks as best we can, alive to the crunching, crackling noise we are making. It is as if my whole body is attuned to danger. A bird flutters out of dense ferns, frightened by our approach, and I jump so badly I almost let off a shot. I've got to get my stupid nerves under control.

Added to which, I'm still trying hard not to look at Ben. Or at least, not to let my eyes *linger* on him. It may be paranoia, but I can't stop thinking that the others are observing us. Especially Heidi. As I scan behind and to my right I catch her looking quickly away. She looks as pale as a ghost even though her face is dripping with sweat.

In the dense foliage, mines, IEDs, snipers, and Vietnam-style booby traps are all a possibility. Every time a twig snaps, my heart leaps and I wonder, am I going to end up like Yugi? Half the platoon is invisible to me in the sap-green shadows and the only thing that holds us together is an occasional line of sight. The radio headsets are hissing quietly. Our eyes scan everywhere — above, to the sides and behind, and especially around our feet.

When Heidi suddenly barks, "COVER!" we all fall to the floor. Except the SEAL next to her. There's a *clack-clack* from his silenced M4 as he fires at something he's seen. He peels off with another SEAL to investigate. They're not gone long but it feels like forever.

"Well?" Ben asks when they return.

"You were right, Lieutenant. We're being followed. And they're good — no sign of them now."

I'm surprised on two counts — by the news that we are being tracked and by the fact that Ben already suspected it.

As we get under way again, creeping ever downward, the musty scent of wet earth rises up from the ground. The flitting of startled birds, screeching and cawing, keeps us all on edge. Somewhere far above our heads a falcon screams. It's hard not to let your imagination run riot with the heat and the constant tension, but there are times when I'm convinced that I see a flash of blue through the flickering branches. Is that Aroush? It isn't there long enough for me to be certain but, if Ben is right, then Aroush and the Young Martyrs are heading back home. I know we're trying to keep off the beaten track but who's to say they wouldn't come this way, too? *She's dangerous . . . bad news . . . always around when someone's about to kick the bucket . . . Husna even thinks she's some kind of messenger from Allah . . .* Ben is searching for her, but I don't know if I really want to see her again.

Soon afterward the ground begins to level off and to feel spongy underfoot. As the covering of trees starts to give way to huge overarching ferns, I pause to adjust the straps on my backpack. Ben gives us the signal to spread out a little more. Husna doesn't bother to wait for me, he forges on ahead with Ben. A strange relief begins to wash over me. Maybe it is gratitude that we have made it through the oppressive trees unscathed, or just that I'm enjoying the occasional shaft of sunlight on my face. Whatever the reason, I can't excuse my lapse of concentration because, as a gentle breeze lifts the fern fronds above my head, Husna lets out a horrible scream and disappears into the earth just in front of Ben's feet.

21

I DON'T KNOW HOW BEN MANAGES TO REACT SO quickly. Before I can blink or even shout for help, he lunges for the boy's shirt collar. He's a millisecond too late and finds himself teetering on the brink of a deep pit, struggling to steady his foothold.

I grab his waist and heave him back. That is when I notice the far too deliberate and regular set of leaves at his feet, and below them a pit set with vicious rusted-iron spikes. And Husna is lying facedown on them. It's a mantrap.

At first I think the boy is not moving at all, then I see his torso expanding and contracting, slowly. Chip and Gizmo are nearest to us, and crash through the undergrowth to help.

Just behind them, Hammed comes into view, his voice full of concern. "What is happen?"

There's no need to answer him. He can see for himself when he reaches the pit.

Ben tells Carlos to set up a perimeter, but the sergeant is already organizing the SEALs, and at my back Heidi is covering us.

I focus all my attention on Husna. Is he impaled on the spikes? My heart is pounding against my chest wall like it's trying to get out. But I'm the medic on scene. I have to do something. Trying to keep my voice steady I call out, "Husna?"

His voice comes back, muffled and weak, "Ellie. Help."

The plea sends us into a frenzy of action. The pit is a bit longer than a tall man and about as wide as my outstretched arms. To our right there is a bigger gap between the sidewall and the first row of spikes. Perhaps where the people who made the trap got out. Ben and Chip lower themselves gingerly down the sides, squeezing and forcing their way through the spikes. Gizmo is too big to get in so he crouches nearby, ready to help me. A bitter, rank smell is rising from the trap as the guys lift aside the loose sticks and ferns that once covered it.

I'm thinking through everything I've been taught about this kind of injury and realizing how little I actually took in. All I can remember is: *Don't remove the foreign body, the patient might bleed to death.* I tell the guys, "If he's impaled, I need to know. Don't do anything unless I say."

Ben is near the boy's head now. "Husna," he asks gently, "you OK?"

There is no answer.

"I can't see any blood," Ben calls up.

"You sure?"

Chip ducks his head under Husna's torso to check. When he comes back out, he spits, wipes his face with the back of his sleeve, and looks up at me. His face is white. When he's able to compose himself he manages to croak, "We're sure."

"OK, then, you can lift him. But if you think any of the spikes have gone in, or he screams, just stop everything and keep him supported."

The guys slide their arms under Husna's torso and slowly, carefully lift him free. As they do so a shower of black, crawling insects fall from him to the bottom of the pit and scurry into the shadows. When he's clear of the spikes, Husna shakes his head violently.

I can see Chip's teeth are clenched while he holds Husna above his head, and he's trying not to look at the swarming insects. Some of them are dropping down his sleeves, but he keeps a tight hold on the boy muttering, "Bugger, bugger," over and over.

Ben handles it like it's just another training day. He shakes his head as the disturbed insects land squirming on it. I wonder if there's anything that could faze him.

When Gizmo and I take Husna from them, we can see why the boy didn't move and what is churning Chip's stomach. He had fallen on a previous victim. The body is still there, rotting, having sunk down the spikes in its death throes, and probably even farther after Husna's impact. Some of the points have come right through its rotting flesh and were separated from Husna by nothing more than a millimeter of threadbare cotton. If he had moved, his body weight alone would have been enough to impale him. The thing he fell on is gross. In places its black flesh is falling away to reveal stained bones and it is crawling with white grubs. Chip is dancing gingerly between the spikes, shaking his sleeves and slapping his arms.

To my horror Husna spits out a stringy mouthful of blood when we get him to his feet.

I'm getting my pack off and am about to start probing his scrawny frame for injuries when he gives me a bloody smile. One of the spikes has knocked a tooth out. I remember that flash of blue I saw in the woods — was it Aroush? How close he came to death. Should I have taken it as a warning . . . ?

My training kicks in. "How're you feeling? Sick? Dizzy?"

Husna shakes his head, puzzled. "Dizzy — what is this?"

The way he says it makes us both laugh. I grab him and steal a grateful hug until he pulls away from me. "It doesn't matter."

Below us Ben and Chip are looking at the body, trying to find ID. It looks like it was a male, dressed in typical Afghan fashion. From the way the body fell the guy must have been heading in the opposite direction to us, away from the mountains. After a minute or so they give up the search and make their way to the side of the pit to get out. That's when I spot something under the layer of ferns that Husna's fall must have disturbed. It looks like a leather strap.

Ben is nearest so I point it out to him. "Lieutenant, wait. Over there!"

He follows the direction of my arm and manages to lean down far enough to grab it. When he pulls, one end breaks away so he tugs gently on the other and, after a bit of gentle work, it comes free. It is a small leather bag. Ben opens it. Inside I can see an old pistol — perhaps Russian — and a sealed yellowing envelope. Ben doesn't open it even though we are all desperate to know what is inside — we need to move. But I do catch a glimpse of the name on the front before he slips it into his jacket. Whoever was delivering it had no need of an address. In neat handwriting is one word: *Macallum*.

We stay just long enough to make the trap safe by impaling any logs we can find on the end of each of the remaining spikes and destroying what is left of the covering. We don't have time to fill the pit in, but at least nobody's going to get seriously hurt if they stumble across it. All the time I'm burning with the desire to see what's inside that envelope. It's from Bella to her father. There's no doubt in my mind — the handwriting on the envelope was the same as the writing on the back of Farshad's photograph. I wonder if Ben will ever share the contents with anyone. Maybe he's worried about what it might say. Whether it's too sensitive.

When we are done, I notice Ben making a beeline for Heidi. She looks like she's been burned when he touches her shoulder and asks her to join him. When she stands up, there's this moment between them, like neither knows who should move first. Then Ben steps aside and lets her walk stiffly in front of him to a point where they can see the lay of the land. I hear him tell her we are going to head for the river and use it as cover, moving upstream for a few miles until we are just below Husna's village. At first Heidi's responses are clipped, but she gradually seems to relax because Ben manages to keep everything so professional and matter-of-fact. He's trying to help her. Awkwardly, it's true, but he's a man. I'm touched. While they are debating the best way to stay out of view as we approach Husna's village, I find Carlos and redo his dressings. There's no way I want river water in that wound.

It's not long before we are off again. Husna and I go up front with the lieutenant once more, and after forty minutes of cutting our way through chest-high undergrowth we emerge on the lush banks of the river. One by one we drop into the cool water and walk knee-deep along it for another hour or so. When we go through the deeper bits, I hope Carlos's dressing is holding up. The riverbed is mostly shale and rock so it's firm underfoot but slippery in places where the water slows and pools. Beds of tall, waving reeds hide us from prying eyes, but the surprised, splashing retreat of the wildlife keeps us all on edge.

Several times Ben has to take Husna onto his shoulders because the water gets too deep for him, and I find myself wondering if there is a change in their relationship. Husna does not let his guard down completely but since the man-trap his body language has been totally different around the American. He no longer pulls away if Ben touches him and when the boy has to be lifted above the waters he manages the indignity with an unconvincing frown.

As we round a wide, rock-strewn bend in the river, a distinctive jagged mountain peak comes into view. I recognize it instantly. It brings back the memory of cordite, smoke, the bitter tang of blood, and Aroush looking through that burning window.

"That's the mountain from Farshad's photograph," I say to Ben.

"Husna?" Ben looks at the boy for confirmation.

He stands there, looking at it. After a long pause he nods and points to the right of the river. "Through fields to Saray."

Ben gives the signal and we follow Husna another hundred meters or so and into an irrigation ditch that has been cut from the river into a narrow, flat section of land. After a few more minutes we clamber out of it into a field of tall, leafy poppies.

Chip points two fingers at his eyes and tells me in a whisper, "Keep 'em peeled, Buffy. Up here poppies mean Taliban.

They make the villagers farm them instead of food crops, so keep your wits about you."

I'm grateful for the warning and my eyes are everywhere as we walk through the field. The saw-edged leaves brush gently along my thighs and the seed-bearing stalks rise like toffee apples on a stick to just above my waist. After the cover of the river we are exposed again in these cultivated, level plantations. Water from my soaking trousers trickles down my legs and the cold, clinging material chafes my thighs. It leaves them sore, but it helps to focus my mind. I'm discovering that, as strange as it might sound, discomfort is good in a war zone. It keeps you on edge. Then I'm thinking that I've been on edge since the day I got here — without wet trousers. I know if I ever make it home I'm going to be a nervous wreck.

Wordlessly, Husna guides us along narrow goat tracks through the poppy fields and up the slope, rounding a steep outcrop of rock. Beyond it the green stuff gives way to the dry, rocky landscape I remember from the photograph. Paths worn by the passage of human feet wind ever higher, and then we reach a plateau. Husna comes to an abrupt stop.

In front of us tumbled, blackened walls are all that remain of Husna's mountain community, Saray. Fourteen or fifteen houses used to stand here and now all that is left is the telltale scatter pattern of bomb-blast rubble. The village has literally been blown to oblivion. You don't need to be Sherlock Holmes to work out what happened.

22

I TAKE IN THE DESTRUCTION. MY BREATH IS RAGGED.

Ben turns to me, then to Hammed and Husna. For the first time since I met him he is visibly shaken. "This was done by drones, Husna?"

His eyes wet with tears, Husna blinks and points along the valley back in the direction of the base and the coalition-held area. "Drones come over this hill. Husna and Farshad see it from this place." He points back down the hill to a small group of pine trees. Then he wipes his face and nose with his arm.

We can all see his story is confirmed by the direction of the blasts. I can almost hear every one, see the spouts of fire, blackened wood and brick falling back to earth along the line of attack. Below us and a little off the main path Gizmo, Chip, and Heidi are checking out a couple of buildings that are still whole enough to be used by insurgents. The SEALs go on ahead to check the high ground.

"So boy's story is true?" Hammed has kept his peace, but he's angry now.

We can't answer him.

Husna points to a couple of crumbling walls. "This one was school."

It isn't much more than two corners of what used to be a large, rectangular room. A dead fig tree has fallen onto the remains. Perhaps it once stood outside a window, planted there for shade. I imagine the schoolroom in the days before the bombing, filled with rows of dusty rugs, a mullah sitting cross-legged near the wall and the singsong voices of children chanting verses from the Qur'an to his gruff accompaniment.

A movement among the rubble and a dull *clang!* have us dropping to a firing position. My finger twitches over the trigger and I have no idea I am holding my breath until a goat emerges from the roofless building next to the schoolroom and bleats at us. For a minute I consider shooting it just to relieve the tension.

Chip grins at me. "Anyone fancy a kebab?"

He's actually mad enough to do it, too. The goat bleats again — more insistently, as if it understands English — and trots off in the opposite direction, stopping to nibble at some tough knots of grass.

It's late afternoon by the time we have checked that Saray is clear of IEDs and booby traps. There is pretty good visibility up here and some protection from attack if whoever is following us is watching, so Ben gives the order to set up camp and we busy ourselves digging in defensive positions and throwing up the tents. When everything is done, I find my eyes sweeping across the devastated village, picturing what it must have been like when it was full of people. Bella Macallum would have walked on this very spot. And I feel anger rising in me at the thought that coalition forces could have been responsible for the destruction. No one in the coalition could have intended this to happen. Husna has to be wrong. There has to be another explanation.

My head is starting to spin so I'm almost grateful to Heidi when she tells me to scout out a good observation point above the village. The SEALs are already setting up a gun position there but Ben has told her he wants one of us on lookout a little higher up. So I leave Husna staring at the poppy field and hope I can get things straightened out in my head.

At the top of the village, a cliff overhangs the path. It curves down to a pile of four huge boulders and I sit with my back to one in a position where I can see both the SEALs and the remains of the village. There is a wall just off the path that will be ideal for Heidi's lookout position. I shade my eyes with my hand to scan for danger points. Warmed by the sun, the rock feels hot against my back. My gun lies across my lap and I keep my hand near the trigger while I watch the afternoon sun paint the head of the valley and the sparkling river with light. I give it a few minutes but it's not helping. I'm too restless and it's stupid to think I can sit up here like I'm sightseeing. I'm just about to get up when Ben drops by my side.

"Need to think, huh?"

"Yes . . . no . . . I don't know. I'm too screwed up about all this." I gesture toward the village.

Ben shakes his head. It's obvious he's finding it tough, too. And there's another thing that's bugging me. I have to tell him.

"Ben . . . I think I might have seen Aroush back in the woods. Just before Husna fell . . ."

"Why didn't you —"

"Say anything? I don't know. I'm mad at myself. It was just a flash of blue — could have been anything."

"Don't beat yourself up about it. We'll find her if she's here. Just don't be afraid to speak up. About anything, all right? Out here details are important."

"OK." I look at him, wondering if I can tell him that I think she was warning me again, but it feels too freaky. One step away from consulting tea leaves.

He takes the envelope from his jacket. "I think it's time to have a look at this, don't you? Maybe it will shed some light on what was going on here."

As I watch him tear the envelope open and pull out a wad of folded yellow sheets, I'm really nervous. I can't believe that he trusts me enough to share this. He unfolds the sheets carefully and a small newspaper clipping falls out. It is stained with brown marks and the stains form a weird geometric pattern across the folds. When he's looked at the clipping, Ben hands it to me in silence and turns to the other sheets.

It's a photograph of a smartly turned-out man shaking hands with a smiling woman outside the UN building in New York. In the margin, in the same neat writing that was on the envelope, is a note: *Zalmai Khan, Afghan interior minister and head of the newly formed Afghan security force, meeting US Secretary of State. Hope she washed her hand afterward.*

"This is Bella Macallum's writing," I say.

"How can you possibly —"

"I've seen it before. The message on Farshad's photograph."

"That makes sense," Ben flicks through the sheets and examines them. The first one seems to be some kind of multicolored map. "These are photocopies of mining surveys of the area around Sabz — geological maps. Seems they were done for the Afghan interior ministry." He points to the ministry stamp at the top right corner of the first sheet.

We look through the rest of them, but they're full of meaningless graphs and projected costs — and certain sections have been blocked out in black marker pen. One thing draws our attention. A small area on one of the weird maps has been circled, and it's next to some very big numbers. The village of Saray is right in the center of the circle.

"There's no cover note?"

Ben exhales slowly. "Too dangerous. I guess the poor guy who fell in that pit was keeping the real message up here." He taps the side of his head.

"Why do you think she used snail mail?"

"No Internet, no phone lines. A journalist like her would have had good reason. And she obviously trusted this guy with her life."

I shiver. "None of this ever reached the general, then. I'll bet the messenger was someone close to her — a family friend or relative. Are you going to call Macallum?"

His face is drained of color. "Not yet. We're very vulnerable up here. Anything we do too hastily could compromise the mission or put us all in danger."

"Husna's drones — the attack — maybe all that was to do with this."

"I'm not going to speculate."

"But what if it was our own side? If the military could do this, what the hell are we doing here?"

His reply is clipped. "We're here to do what we do every day. We focus on the job."

"Yeah? Well, I thought our job was to help these people, not to kill them."

I've stumped him. He just looks at me. "Ellie, let's not fight. We both want the same thing here."

I hope he's right.

"We're gonna sit on this for a while longer, OK?" he says, getting to his feet. "I've got a feeling there is more to find. For the moment, this is just between you and me."

Before the light starts to fail, Ben, Husna, Hammed, and I scour the area around Aroush's house for any evidence of the family that lived here. All that is left of it now is a couple of rooms. I can just make out where the front door was, facing the valley. Outside I can see the cluster of rocks where Farshad and Aroush had been playing in the photo. A blackened crater lies next to them now.

"Kitchen here," Husna tells us. And his words are confirmed by the presence of a rusting gas bottle, blown virtually inside out and lying on its side. It is still connected to a battered portable stove.

Hammed picks it up and turns it over thoughtfully in his huge hands. Then his expression changes from doubt to confusion, and he turns to Husna. "Where are remains? People die here. Should be bones . . ."

He has a point. It's strangely comforting that the Afghan is finding it as hard to get his head round this as the rest of us are. We all look at Husna.

"Young Martyrs come back and all is gone."

"Someone hid the bodies?" I ask him. "Where?"

The boy replies with his trademark shrug. "Some men still here. Farshad want kill them. Say he can get many gun. By time Young Martyrs have them, men is gone. Many, many day Farshad and Young Martyrs look for them. We find them by Darzab."

The gun battle we stumbled on. "McQueen thought they were Afghan security . . ."

"Not know," Husna tells me flatly.

Ben asks, "Husna, when the village was attacked, did you see what happened to Aroush's parents? Her mother?"

There's no response. He's struggling because he thinks he's told us too much already. I crouch by him and take his hand. "It's important, Husna."

When he replies, he'll only look at me. "Night before bombing Taliban take her. Farshad's father send children away because village is going to fight — then bombs come."

Hammed claps his hands. "Taliban here! Then Americans bomb village. This make sense."

"Were the Taliban here the day the drones attacked, Husna?" I wonder.

He shakes his head. But it is clear he has no idea why any of this happened, either.

There's nothing more to see at Bella's house so we move on. I take a look in the schoolroom while Ben and Hammed root around in the debris outside. There's nothing much to be found there, either. The gray branches of the fallen fig tree obscure most of the rubble, but one part of the wall was clearly used for displaying the children's work — a crayon picture on torn, smudged paper clings to it, fluttering gently in the breeze. When I look closer, the picture is chilling. Angry stick men with machine guns guard a field of bright red poppies. In the middle of the field one of the guards seems to be kicking a villager who lies at his feet. I turn down one of the flapping corners and see that it has been drawn on the back of an old map.

"Seen this?" I call outside to Ben. "Looks like the villagers were definitely being forced to grow those poppies."

Husna comes in to look, too. "Aroush help look after young ones for Mullah Behzad in here, they draw poppies." Then he points at the villager in the picture, and what he says sends a shiver down my spine. "That father of Aroush."

Ben's face flushes with anger. "Why were they beating him?"

"He not like what they do. Whole village is hungry and he tell them. Picture is made two week before bombs."

No wonder the Young Martyrs are fighting both sides. The Taliban were making them farm opium and we bombed the hell out of them for some reason.

"*If* what you say is true, believe me, we're gonna get to the bottom of it," Ben says. I can tell he's trying to keep his voice level. Like me, he's mad that all our hard work building trust out here could be undermined by our own forces.

I don't want to consider the possibility that coalition troops massacred Husna's family, either, but I know I'm not going to run from the truth even if it kills me. I made Husna a promise and I'm going to keep it.

Husna turns away and flicks his battered toy onto a flat section of the wall. It spins and wobbles onto its side and drops to the floor just as Carlos arrives. He picks it up and Husna holds out his hand expectantly, but the American scrutinizes it for a moment.

"Where did you get this?"

The boy is suspicious. "Nowhere."

Carlos looks at it again. "Lieutenant, do you know what this is?"

"Should I?"

The sergeant passes it over Husna's head, much to the boy's disgust. "It's a missile gyro. Part of an AGM-65 Maverick guidance system."

Ben shows me. "How can you be so sure?"

"I've seen a million of these things. Look at the bottom!"

I turn it over and can just make out the word *Honeywell*, embossed on the circular rim.

"That's a Honeywell gyro, made in Phoenix, Arizona. And guess what, the AGM-65s can be carried by Predator ground-attack drones."

The boy's eyes are wide as I give it back to him. "Husna, this is really important. Where did you get this?"

"Here!" The boy grabs my hand and leads us back down to the poppy field just below the village.

We wade after him through the stems to a point near where the field gives way to that small stand of pine trees. The boy falls to his knees and scours the ground with his hands. Hammed drops next to him. Within a few minutes Husna cries out in triumph, holding a battered piece of metal in the air. "I find it inside this!"

Carlos takes it from him. He looks at Ben and shakes his head. "That's it. That's part of the casing of an AGM-65."

I want to cry when I see the desolate look on Husna's face. He knows what this means, but it is a hollow victory for him. Everyone he loved is still dead.

"Allahu Akbar," Hammed grunts, landing a gentle cuff on the back of Husna's head.

The boy echoes his words, his face pale with grief. Then Hammed actually places a comforting hand on the boy's shoulder and pulls him to his side. Husna's eyes fill with tears as he turns his toy over in his hands. I imagine it must be like holding the blade that cut his family to pieces, so I take it from him before he is tempted to hurl it into the river. He does not object.

"This is your proof, Husna. Whoever did this cleaned everything else up, but they missed this."

Chip finds me in the bombed-out schoolroom later. I'm taking the opportunity to look at the picture one last time before the light fails. He sits down next to me and sighs heavily.

"You OK, Buffy?"

I don't speak because I know he is not interested in the answer. I remember the MCR song "I'm Not Okay." I'm not OK. I'm not OK yay freaking yay. Nowhere near. It's not Chip's fault though. He's just making small talk while he tries to phrase whatever it is he really came to say, so I bury my anger at what happened here, put my arm around his broad shoulders, and pat his back.

We are both silent for a while, then he asks, "Do you ever think about Yugi?"

I swallow the grief before it can surface, but I say, "No. I can't." It's a lie. So much for the honesty I value so much. I do think about him a lot, especially now, especially here. I wonder what he died for and whether it was worth it, but I can't tell Chip that.

"It's weird how we can be best pals with someone one minute and the next it is as if they never existed. Makes you wonder what would happen if . . . you or I, you know . . ."

"Has to be that way," I manage. "I didn't know him for long but I'm never going to forget him, you know?"

Chip nods and we both wipe away a tear and sit there for a while.

Eventually he gets up and says, "Thanks, Buffy. You're spot-on. If . . . *it* happens — you know. I just want you to know that I'm sorry about what happened when we met. I can be an arse sometimes."

That forces a laugh out of me. "Yes, you can."

After he disappears into the darkness I let the tears come for real, hot and angry. But they aren't just for Yugi. They're for Bella Macallum, for the people who lived here, for the children.

23

NOW NIGHT HAS FALLEN I SHOULD TRY TO GET some rest but I can't sleep, and so I sit down to clean and oil my rifle. My mind wanders like a lost child. Someone allowed that air strike to happen. Was it an accident or deliberate? If the coalition is as bad as the Taliban, if it can target innocent civilians in this tiny mountain village, then, really, what is the point? But I can't let my mind drift. The second it does I get this horrible feeling of certainty creeping over me, filling my head, a feeling that this is where I am going to . . . croak. And if I do, will it all be for nothing?

I watch the Americans and for the first time I notice that they don't mix with our guys much. Even the ones Chip has played poker with. We're like oil and water. Their elite training makes them untouchable and the only things we seem to have in common are a language and our enemy. But could any of them target civilians? I can't believe it. I signed up to help, to make a difference, not to be a part of the problem — and definitely not to kill innocents. If what Husna says is true, I'm going to leave the army. Nothing will stop me.

I'm spinning again. Time to get up.

In our half of the camp Heidi is more animated than I've ever seen her. She's actually laughing with Gizmo over some joke or other, even if she does stop short when she realizes I've noticed them. I put it down to the way Ben has been trying to include her in the decision-making. He's probably shown her the contents of the envelope, too.

Just so I don't think she's softening, she posts me on sentry duty behind the cover of the wall I reconnoitered near the top of the village. It's not something I relish. I'm so badly twisted up inside by what's happened here that the last thing I need is hours alone with nothing but my thoughts. I get some relief when Carlos comes to check on me. As he walks away, in the dim light cast by a crescent moon I can't help noticing that the sergeant looks like he's not in so much pain. He might even be on the road to recovery. I should be pleased, but I just feel hollow.

It's way past midnight when I hear the dull clatter of rocks behind me. I think the approaching movement must be the relief lookout although part of me can't help wondering if I'm going to see Aroush rising from the shadows instead. But it's better than that. Much better.

I see his cap first, then Ben emerges from the night, kicking aside some rubble to reach me. Soon he's at my side. The warmth of his body is like an aura and I find myself leaning toward it. I don't ask myself why he's here. Or why the ache inside me has suddenly eased.

"You did a good job — with Carlos," he says.

"He seems to be doing OK. Don't you ever sleep?"

He laughs. "Didn't you know? SEALs don't need sleep. Anyway, Carlos is more than OK, thanks to you."

I blush, pleased by the compliment. "Are you sure you really needed to bring him along?"

"Yes, I'm sure."

"It's a nasty wound. I didn't believe I could really help him out here."

"Trust me, we're all capable of more than we think."

I can't help but wonder what he's thinking about all of this destruction. Then I remember his face when Husna was talking about the air strike. "D'you think Macallum knows about what happened here? He went quiet when you told him about it."

Ben's smile disappears. "Maybe."

I realize that he's as screwed up about this as I am. So I try to cut Macallum some slack. "Maybe the general didn't know the full truth, just that something happened and his daughter was at the center of it."

Ben looks at me for a moment. "What's been going on here, Ellie? The SEALs are my life. I can't believe I'm a part of an army that would deliberately bomb innocent civilians. It just doesn't make sense. I know I'm here to find that arms cache and, if I can, to discover what happened to the general's daughter, but there's something much bigger going on. I don't know, what if the US government is involved? I'm not sure I can still tow the line if we sanctioned this. But they wouldn't have sent me here to find out if they knew, would they?"

"I don't think so. I hate all of this, Ben — I hate not knowing. Would it help to go over the evidence again with me? Something might leap out at us."

"You're right." Ben leans next to me with his back to the wall.

I have to stay in position, scanning over the wall.

He takes a deep breath, picking up a stone and throwing it away angrily. It skitters down the hillside. Then he says, "I'll start. We know that there was an air strike on this village by coalition drones."

"Right. But before that, Bella came to Afghanistan as a journalist, married an Afghan called Jahadar, and came to live in this village with him. He already had a boy — Farshad — and she later gave birth to Aroush. For some reason, Bella was taken away by the Taliban just before the bombing."

"At the same time the Taliban were using a cave in this area as a top-secret arms cache and forcing the villagers to farm opium."

"Then there's the photograph of that guy Khan and the mining surveys."

"So there's something valuable in the ground up here, but this is in Taliban territory. No mining company would come here unless they could be sure of protection." Ben throws another stone down the hillside. "And a coalition air strike, Ellie? There has to be a link, but what?"

We go over all we know again and again, scouring our memories for anything that might point to what went on, until Ben finally mutters, "If you ask me, Macallum wants to know what went on as much as we do. Otherwise he wouldn't have sent us."

"OK, we can assume it wasn't him who actually ordered that air strike. He's new in the job. But if someone in the army did it, someone he knows even, can you honestly tell me that you think he wouldn't do everything he could to bury the evidence? Can you say that you know the guy? I mean really know him?"

"As a matter of fact I can. My dad served with him in Iraq. He's a family friend."

"Oh?" I'm derailed, I don't know what to say. Ben knows Macallum that well? No wonder he's finding it so hard to look at this objectively. The information leaves me wondering if Macallum chose Ben for this mission because he knows he can trust him or because he can trust him to be discreet. From what I've seen, though, I prefer to believe Ben has more integrity. "And you think family friends can't . . ."

"Not this one, no." He shakes his head and something inside me melts at his certainty, his loyalty. He watches me silently, then smiles.

"What?"

"You're wasted here, you know that?"

The compliment floors me. I want to throw caution to the wind, to give in to the charisma that draws me to him and takes my breath away — but I'm gripped by a sudden realization and a knot of fear makes my stomach drop. "Ben, Husna could be a target now — he's a witness to the bombing. And if whoever ordered that attack finds out he's alive, and that we've got evidence of drones in the area . . . I have to protect him."

I wonder if it's my imagination or if, when Ben straightens up and we stand there side by side, he really does lean into me. "*You* don't have to protect him, Ellie. We all do. And every one of us is in danger now."

"I know." I'm supposed to be keeping watch but I can't turn away from him. "Really, I should get back . . ."

"Do you know, if this wasn't a war zone," he says quietly, "and you and I weren't . . ."

"You're just trying to shut me up . . ."

"Well, yeah . . ."

". . . by rambling like an idiot." I say it lightly, but now I'm looking right into his eyes and then at the curve of his lips. We can't be more than an inch apart. I think I might actually have stopped breathing.

"I'm not good at this . . ." he mutters at last. "I'm not sure I can do my job with you . . ."

Without thinking — I mean, without thinking *at all* — I put my fingers to his half-open mouth and wait there, feeling the warmth of his breath on them and the rise and fall of his chest. My head feels like it is coming apart. I so want him to kiss me, to give in to whatever force is making me fall toward him, but I'm torn. He is, too. I know that. All I can do is watch his eyes drop to my lips. It's like time has been suspended.

How we both pull away I will never know, but when we do finally part I feel like I'm waking from some strange dream, scared that I have overstepped the mark and nothing I can say will make it right. The harsh reality of our surroundings seems to pour into the gap between us like a flood, extinguishing the flame completely. All that is left is the pounding of my heart in my ears. We stare at each other.

He looks shocked. "I'm sorry, I shouldn't have . . ."

"No . . . no . . . really, I'm . . . um . . ."

And all the time I'm wondering if I sound as stupid as I feel, and why he is apologizing, and if he regrets what just happened, or, rather, didn't just happen. I think I'm about to explode. If we were anywhere else in the world . . .

The shadows return then, pulling at the back of my mind. What if he dies? What if I die? I want to get out of here, to run away, but I can't. I'm stuck here like an idiot because it's my duty. I can barely bring myself to utter the words, "You should go."

For the first time ever, I see him hesitate over a decision. Then, with a nod, he's gone and I'm alone again in the cold black night.

A gunshot cracks and echoes across the valley below me and I'm still looking at the place where Ben disappeared. The camp is suddenly alive with voices. I grab my night-vision goggles and fumble for the switch. *Why the hell wasn't I watching?* Like I don't know why. I'm so stupid. The green light is still so bright that I have to lose valuable seconds blinking away painful tears. I force my eyes to stay open and stare down the glowing hillside. Some of our guys are heading into the poppy field and toward the river. I can't be sure, but I think that there is some movement on the bank opposite. Could be human or animal. It disappears before I can tell which.

While I'm still wrong-footed, a luminous green Heidi virtually careers up the hill into me at full pelt.

"There's been an intruder. Did you see anything?"

"Just a flash."

"He was in the poppy field — you've got clear line of sight from up here."

I don't know how to answer.

She just looks at me. "You were with someone, weren't you? Jackson?"

It's like the woman has some sixth sense. There's no point

lying, so I say, "Yes," and brace myself. But I'm surprised, despite the tone of her voice, at how fragile she looks.

With an incredible effort she keeps her voice quiet. "What did he want? I hope for your sake it was worth it."

"He wanted to know how Carlos is doing." It isn't a lie, technically.

"And he couldn't have asked the guy himself?" She looks at me, hard. "Just remember, *Private*. This is a job not a high school prom and, in case you hadn't noticed, we're on the front line. So go ahead, screw up the rest of your life, but do it in your own time. Screw up out here and you endanger the team. And then, God help you, you answer to me. Do you understand?"

I nod, feeling miserable for messing up. I'm just hoping that gunshot doesn't mean my lapse of concentration has cost someone's life as well as my peace of mind. For the first time since I got here I truly understand how Heidi must feel.

24

TO MY EVERLASTING RELIEF, NO ONE IS HURT. The gunshot was from one of our guys on sentry duty at the other end of the poppy field, and he missed. But Chip and Gizmo got the intruder. They deposit their captive without ceremony at the feet of the lieutenant. There's no point in anyone sleeping now. We're all too wired.

It is an Afghan security-forces fighter, by the looks of his uniform, and one of his eyes is swelling badly. These guys are supposed to be on our side. *Why are they spying on us?*

"I should treat that," I tell Chip.

He's short with me. "Don't bother, Buffy. He's not going to let you near him anyway."

As if to confirm Chip's words the prisoner scowls at me like he's just found me on the sole of his shoe.

Husna is sitting on one of the rocks nearby, kicking his legs, and Hammed is waiting to interpret. The Afghan watches intently while Ben stoops to read the guy's identity tag, and his face is black with anger.

Ben pulls himself up. "So, what's going on, Omar?"

Hammed barks the question at him.

Omar does not answer, just stares at us defiantly.

"Why are you following us?" Ben asks calmly.

The captive's eyes flash at Husna but he still says nothing.

That's why he was here. He was trying to get the boy. Because Husna is a witness to what happened up here.

"Lieutenant — do you think we should ask him if he's been to Saray before? Like — around the time of the bombing?"

Still angry, Hammed goes ahead and asks him anyway.

Omar spits at Ben and yammers something, his face contorted, his words seething with hatred. Unable to contain himself any longer, Hammed takes a step toward him, raising the back of his hand and swearing in Pashto.

The captive scrambles backward, clearly rattled. Hammed is not a pretty sight when he's angry.

Fortunately for Omar, Ben intervenes before Hammed can land a blow. "What did he say?"

Hammed stands there with his hand raised. "He insult Ellie."

The guy still won't look me in the eye, but he defends my honor. I'm touched.

Chip has been simmering behind me, now he loses it. "Why don't you give me and Gizmo five minutes with him?" he asks, grabbing a handful of Omar's shirt. "This psycho jumped me with a knife." Buttons scatter.

It takes three soldiers to pull Chip back.

Now I feel bad. I noticed the prisoner's black eye but missed the angry red scratch across Chip's windpipe. It's like a shaving cut and must be quite sore. I try to look at it but he bats my hand away. The wound is better left to heal in the air anyway. Chip must have been seconds away from having his throat slit. Somehow he'd managed to fight Omar off. When I think of my lapse on lookout I thank God he did.

Ben shakes his head. "Take it easy, Chip. Hammed, ask him who he is working for. Tell him he'd best answer quickly or we'll leave him alone with Chip here."

The threat seems to focus Omar's mind because he splutters a reply.

"He say he come to clean this place of American filth. To make sure we leave with nothing."

Then the guy shouts a string of bitter, snarling words at Husna, stopping abruptly when Hammed angrily clips the side of his head with his handgun.

Whatever it was he said, it has an instant effect. The boy screams at him and makes a dive for Chip's gun. Gizmo has to lift Husna from the ground and clamp him, still struggling, against his chest. He yells, "Steady! Steady!" until Husna stops kicking.

The look on the boy's face is dark and murderous. Gizmo

puts him back on the ground, gripping his shoulders. Somehow Husna still manages to spit in Omar's face, free one of his arms, and point a shaking finger at him. "I will kill you . . ."

"What was that all about?" Ben asks calmly.

"Says that Husna's mother was a whore and he laughed when she die — was watching bombing with binoculars. Says we will all die, too. Like American controller . . ."

Omar looks at Ben and draws a line across his throat with his index finger.

I'm confused. "American controller?"

"A forward air controller," Ben tells me. "Afghan security forces are trained by the coalition but they can't request a strike on their own — they'd have to use one of our guys. That must have been how the bombing was called in. Some poor sap with a knife at his throat being forced to lie — to tell the air force that Saray was crawling with Taliban. The drone pilots wouldn't have seen civilians — the kids had fled and most of the adults were holed up in the schoolroom."

"The Afghan security forces wanted this village destroyed?"

"Possibly just a renegade unit." When Ben turns to Hammed again his voice is low, dangerous. "Ask him again, who sent him?"

Omar's obviously too afraid to say any more because he clams up. It looks like he'd rather take his chances with Chip than tell us that. As far as he is concerned the interview is over. But he does manage one last dig as Hammed turns his back on him.

Hammed stops in his tracks and translates. "He say that hand of Allah will wipe us all from face of earth."

We don't waste any more time. It's almost dawn so at least there is some light to work by. I pack up my kit and check my gun. Then we wait for Ben's orders. It's clear we need to get out of here. We've got photos and Husna's evidence. They'll have to do. I'm guessing Ben's trying to figure out how to find the arms cache before we leave. That is officially why we're here, after all. There is no sign of Aroush or the Young Martyrs. That'll be another mission now.

I find Husna sitting on the ground by Heidi's tent. She's showing him how the headset radios work. He's wearing her helmet and she presses the button on the side of her rifle. I put my helmet on and Husna's voice crackles in it.

"Young Martyrs need this radio," he says enviously. "Where we get it?"

Everyone in a helmet grins as they hear the boy speak.

Talk of the Young Martyrs ends the game for Heidi. She takes her helmet back and shoos Husna away.

Hammed takes the boy to one side to get him out of her way and shows him how to perform his pre-prayer ablutions with water from a plastic bottle. The Afghan seems to have perfected a high-speed version for war zones, and they fall in a silent rhythm to touch their faces to the floor. Like a mullah and his little disciple.

They manage to finish by the time Ben and Carlos approach us. Hammed clambers to his feet and dusts himself down and Husna copies him, patting small clouds of dust out of his torn trousers with the palms of his hands.

Ben's face is gray with worry and there are dark circles under his eyes. "Last night I sent a recon team ahead to check out the area around the next-nearest village, Chakhi," he tells Heidi, "to see if they can find any clues as to where this arms cache could be."

He throws a quick glance my way and holds it just long enough for me to feel uncomfortable. Thankfully I don't blush like a schoolgirl. The look is hard to decipher, but I'm hoping I didn't hurt him by telling him to leave last night. It's just a matter of timing . . . and rank. We both know this would never work. Especially not here.

Nothing escapes Heidi. She looks at him with dead eyes, disapproving. "And did they find anything?"

"It was deserted, bombed like here, but there was evidence of a recent firefight, too."

"The same Afghan security unit?"

Ben nods. "More than likely — and fighting the Young Martyrs. This unit is a serious problem. They've been trained by the US or the British army, and you can bet they're well equipped. Omar's wearing the uniform of the Afghan security forces, but it's clearly a renegade group. We need to get out of here and forget looking for the arms cache."

And then he says something to Heidi that I shall always love him for. "But if nothing else comes out of this mess we're going to collect as much evidence as we can and get justice for the kids before we go. I know what my guys will want to do. What about yours, Corporal?"

For the first time Heidi smiles at him properly. She nods, and they shake hands like they are making a pact. "Agreed. We'll have to leave the cache," she says. "It's just a shame no one drew us a map."

It is then that my mind turns a somersault. I'm back in the schoolroom, looking at that picture, turning down the corner . . .

"The picture in the schoolroom," I say.

Everyone turns to me.

  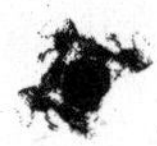

Soon we're back in what was left of the schoolroom. A wind devil rises, twisting like a mini tornado among the blasted remains, lifting clouds of dirt into our eyes and ears and for us to crunch between our teeth. It is like someone has slowed down time, made every movement an effort, like I am a stick-man in that drawing. The yellowing picture is lying in the rubble and I'm holding my breath as Ben stoops to pick it up.

He turns it over. On the back is another US Geological Survey map, just like the one in Bella's envelope, and a small, round circle has been drawn on it. A luminous yellow highlight a few centimeters above Saray. Farshad's cave.

25

IT TAKES US FORTY-FIVE MINUTES TO FIND IT. BEN leaves Heidi and most of his men defending the village. Gizmo and Chip are with Husna and me, and Ben walks with his sergeant. Carlos is carrying a huge backpack. It's a tough walk in searing heat past evergreen trees too malnourished to offer much shade and over rough, stony ground — all of it uphill. It is Carlos who spots the entrance. I can see nothing more than a cleft cliff face, with a loose scattering of rocks and shale.

"This is it?" Ben looks at the map, then at Carlos.

"I'd say so. A gap in the rock that's been filled in by an explosion, see?"

None of us does.

Husna is excited. “Yes! Farshad hide cave with explosion. He say he bury it like we bury Taliban and American scum.”

I give him a look, and he shrugs it off.

Carlos runs his hands over the cliff face. “About twenty minutes?” he says to Ben.

Ben looks at his watch. “You’ve got ten.”

In the end it takes Carlos only five minutes to lay his charges and set up a safe zone behind an outcrop. Sweat is pouring from his forehead and running in rivulets down his face when he finally runs back to us in the safe zone. The sergeant takes a well-worn gray box from beneath his armpit and the antenna wobbles erratically as he presses a couple of buttons on the front. When he turns the key to prime it he grins at me.

“Santa Maria, I owe you, Ellie. I feel great,” he says.

I laugh. “You don’t look it.”

“You Brits got some secret potion thing, eh?”

“Yeah,” I say, “but don’t tell anyone — it’s experimental.”

“Your secret’s safe with me.” Carlos smiles, handing me the detonator and wiping his forehead with the back of his dusty arm. “Here, you do it. I need to sit down.”

He gives me the nod and I press the button.

There is a mild *WHUMP*, a small gray dust cloud, and the mountainside spews a neat scattering of angular boulders.

“Is that it?” I say.

Husna spits on the ground in disgust.

Carlos mutters, "Philistines," but he's smiling.

I'm looking at Carlos with new eyes and he knows it. He's shifted tons of rock and there's no sign that even the birds noticed the explosion, let alone Omar's renegades. This is why Ben dragged his wounded sergeant out here and halfway up a mountain.

We clamber down from our safe zone and make our way over the rough, uneven ground to the mouth of the cave. The opening is as tall and narrow as a cruise missile, and dust falls down it like a ghostly waterfall. Walking through it is like passing through a gray curtain into another world. Only one person at a time can enter so Ben posts Chip and Gizmo as sentries, and takes Carlos and me with our flashlights to check for booby traps.

The roof of the cave is not much higher than the entrance, but it is wide and goes back a long way. It is full of packing cases. Many of them have been opened and the lids have been stacked against one of the sidewalls, where they lean untidily with a couple of rusty old crowbars. A few of the open cases have been ransacked. There is a jumble of Russian Kalashnikovs and magazines for them, and an open box of landmines. No adult would have left them piled that way. I'm nervous just looking at them.

"There are enough weapons in here to start World War Three," Ben mutters as we probe the darkest corners of the cave with our flashlights. "Rocket launchers, guns, ammo, antitank missiles — most of them courtesy of Uncle Sam."

He points to the telltale star on the side of some of the cases. Some of the others have Russian and Chinese writing on them.

"Looks like whoever they were intended for never made use of them though," I observe. "I wonder why?"

Chip sticks his head inside and whistles appreciatively when he sees the cases. He shouts, "Oi!" when Husna takes the opportunity to slip through his legs.

He runs to my side. "Farshad kill the Taliban men who hide this. Was big secret. He kill them before they tell others where to find cave." Then he starts rummaging in the box of mines like he's found some new toys.

The way they clunk together heavily scares me. "Husna, leave those!" I wait until his grubby little hands are out of the box before I can breathe again. "Wasn't Farshad ever going to come back here for more?"

"Yes."

"Then why blow up the entrance?"

"Only way to hide it. Can blow it open again."

"With all these mines in here? I don't think so. Not unless you know what you're doing."

Husna makes a face like I must be mad to suggest Farshad might not have known what he was doing. They must have thought they were indestructible.

"Ellie, look."

I look where he is pointing. There is what appears to be a shallow grave, piled with rocks.

A few minutes later, with the four of us shifting the boulders, I uncover the white bones of a hand still joined with tendons and cartilage. As we work, we uncover some parts of the body where the flesh is still rotting. The smell makes me heave. It soon becomes clear that we've found the sad remains of Bella Macallum. There's no doubt in my mind it's her. So that's what Farshad meant when he told me, *I bury her . . . in cave*. There is a charred old teddy bear under her left arm and photographs of Farshad, Aroush, and Jahadar in a pile at her feet. Ben flicks through them carefully.

My voice echoes around us. "What do you think happened to Bella's husband?"

"They wouldn't have been interested in him," Carlos mutters. "Probably shot him in the woods and kicked the body down the hill. Her . . . they would have questioned her for hours."

The sergeant sounds disturbingly sure of himself. I wonder how much of this sort of thing he's seen. Judging by the single bullet wound in her temple, under the straggling remains of her hair, it looks like Bella was eventually executed. It might even have happened on this very spot.

On her chest the corner of a manila folder peeps out from beneath the rubble and, as Carlos and I lift the last few boulders off her torso, I see there is a diary resting on top of it. Ben leaves me to brush off the dust and open it up. He squats next to me, looking over my shoulder. It's crammed full of entries and scraps of paper with notes scrawled on them, a real mess.

"Perhaps Farshad witnessed his mother's execution and that was why he killed the Taliban guards. That might explain why all this is still here, too . . ."

"There's no time to do this now," Ben tells me. "Carlos, get back out there and see if there's any sign of the Afghans. We need to get this stuff away from here . . ."

Carlos is already moving. "I'm on my way."

"What are we going to do with all this?" I help Ben to gather it up.

"The forensic stuff will have to wait, but I want the documents in Macallum's hands yesterday."

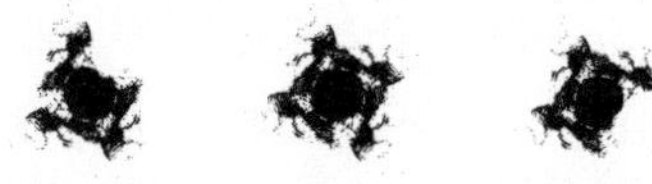

When we emerge from the cool of the cave, the sun is scorching. We get back down to the village a lot quicker than we came and now there is an urgency to everything we do. Ben wants us out of here before the renegades try anything.

As we separate to get our kit, Ben calls, "Nice work, Nielson!"

I turn at the doorway of Bella Macallum's house. He's standing by the schoolroom, and he flashes me a smile that takes my breath away. But before he can give the orders to break camp, there is a delicate skittering of shale behind him and a small, slim figure appears just beyond the schoolroom wall, half obscured by the gray, twisted branches of the dead fig tree. She ducks beneath one of the branches, her feet hardly disturbing the dust, and stops.

There is no mistaking the blue dress, the tangle of black hair, the haunting green eyes. But for the first time she's smiling. I get it — she just wanted us to find her mother. And now she's happy. Was that always her intention? To find someone who cared, to lead us toward the mountains, to Saray?

I'm about to call out to her when I notice her smile fade. Suddenly her attention is riveted on Ben. Slowly, carefully, she starts to walk toward him.

It's like someone has thrown ice-cold water down my spine.

No . . .

There's a pressure building in my head, throbbing in my temples. I'm fighting black spots that swell and swim before my eyes and threaten to blot out the sun completely. Just like it did when Farshad and Yugi died . . . She was there . . . *Not Ben. It can't be Ben . . .*

Aroush's hair falls over her face in a breath of wind so that all I can see is one pale, riveting eye. A tear is forming in it. It's about to drop.

I open my mouth to shout a warning, but the words don't even leave my lips.

Ben looks at me with a question. Just at me. The sun glints briefly off his identity tag, and then all hell breaks loose.

26

I DON'T HEAR THE EXPLOSION. I JUST FEEL MYSELF lifted from the ground and I'm thrown into the remains of Bella's house like a rag doll. I lie there, breathless, wondering if I'm dead, until my eyes begin to focus on the remains of the gas cylinder. My ears whine and howl, and then the world rushes back in with a roar.

Rounds whizz all around me, thudding into the walls and showering me with razor-sharp shards. *Ben . . .*

Rolling onto my stomach, I push my helmet back, and see him. The mortar has thrown him into a gap in the schoolroom wall and wedged him in by his heavy backpack.

I scramble to my feet, and begin stumbling drunkenly toward him. The air is thick around me — black like bitumen — and my legs scream with the effort of moving. Sweat sticks my clothes to me, hampering my every step.

Ben's face flushes with anger when he sees me approaching, and the sinews in his neck pull taut like bowstrings. "GET DOWN, ELLIE!" he yells while he struggles to free himself. "GET THE HELL DOWN! I CAN DO THIS MYSELF!"

Ignoring the thud and splutter of incoming rounds at my feet, I pull out my knife and stagger toward him. But Heidi is closer than I am and she's scrambling to help him, too. Ben is struggling with his pack, yelling at her to go away, but she does not listen to him, either. She is already there and sawing through one of his straps with her bayonet.

As I leap over a jumble of boulders I'm expecting every *whizz!*, every *crack!* to take me down. I pray it will hit me, not Ben. But Aroush was walking toward him. Her eyes were fixed on him. She's not of this world and, wherever she is, death is not far behind. It's coming and I can't get to him in time.

Heidi sees Aroush, still behind the schoolroom, and her face turns white. She shouts in faltering Pashto, *"Dha sta na dhay! DHA . . . STA NA . . . DHAY!"* as she works frantically to free Ben, shielding him with her body. They are both sitting targets.

All I can do is watch in silent horror as a round whips past me, scalding my cheek, and punches a crimson hole in Heidi's back.

All I can do is grab her shoulders and pull her to me.

All I can do is hold her and feel the warm life pulse out of her, soaking my fatigues and sticking them to my breast.

As I struggle to take her weight I can see that Heidi has managed to cut Ben free enough for him to twist out of the remaining strap. The bullet has passed right through Heidi and hammered a bloody tear in Ben's backpack. It's still wedged in the wall. He's missed death by a millisecond.

Ben tries to help me catch Heidi as she falls, and we stumble together onto the jagged floor. A storm of automatic fire clatters around us. Ben rolls Heidi onto her back and I can see the front of her sticky combat jacket tug away from his when he releases her. I push him away and kneel beside her to look at that terrible hole, and all the time my tears are falling and mingling with the blood that oozes from it. We both know that she is going to die. I press down on it hard with the palm of my hand.

She asks me, "Am I hit?" in a hoarse whisper, and I can't answer her. "Nielson, I can't feel my arms."

"It's OK. I'm going to help you," I tell her, fighting back the tears and pulling at my pack with my free hand, trying to find the hemorrhage gel. "You're going to be just fine. Now lie still — don't move."

"I've been too hard on you . . ."

Heidi's eyelids flutter like she's losing consciousness. I slap her cheek gently to get her to focus. "Stay with me, OK?"

Ben looks grim — he has to lead his men and leave me

alone with her. The air around us is thick with hot, cracking shards of metal.

"I'll be fine!" I shout above the din, finding the gel. "Just go."

He nods, but instead he kneels next to us, giving orders to his guys through his neck mic. Next thing I know, Carlos is scrambling through the ruins to him.

I don't see any more. I release pressure on the wound so I can tear Heidi's jacket away. Her lips move. They're turning blue. At first I think she's angry with me, but then I realize her unseeing eyes are flicking left and right, trying to locate my face. "Leave me, Ellie. Please!"

"Don't be stupid . . ." I begin.

She doesn't have much strength but she's trying to fight me off. Her voice is little more than a whisper now. "I know I'm going to die. When Toni died . . . it should have been me. It should always have been me."

"You can't say that, Heidi!"

"It's what I was saying to Aroush . . . *Dha sta na dhay.* It means 'This one's not yours.' *Me*, not Ben. Is he OK?"

"You saved him." I pull apart her jacket while she's distracted and get pressure on the wound again.

Heidi smiles. "My life for his . . . Yes, that's how it should be." I open my mouth to protest, but she whispers with all her remaining strength, "Go! For God's sake, don't let this be for nothing. Not now . . ."

Another wave of incoming fire almost drowns out her words. I cover her body with mine until I realize that it's not aimed at us. Gizmo is running across the hill just below the schoolroom and he's with Hammed, who is dragging Omar along with him in a headlock. They seem to be aiming for the same cover as Chip. To my relief I see that Husna is already crouching there. I shoulder my SA80 to give them covering fire. There's no hope for Heidi. I should do what she says and go help them. Shouldn't I? For a second I'm caught in indecision, my finger on the trigger. Should I try to save the life of the woman who has made my life hell, or should I do what she wants and let her die for the team? There is no real choice for me. There never was. I put my gun down.

"I'm not leaving you, Heidi. I'm part of your team now, and this is my job."

I grab a pouch of hemorrhage gel with my free hand. Trying to ignore the bitter tang of her blood as I tear the pack open with my teeth, I spit out the tab and pour the white powder into the gaping exit wound in her chest and apply pressure again. It swells and slows the crimson fountain to a trickle, filling me with a false hope, but when I fumble at her collar for a pulse, the feeble rhythm of life is fading to nothing beneath my fingertips. I swear at her, slap her face again, and pull back her lifeless eyelids, watching helplessly as her pupils relax to wide black holes.

There is no point attempting CPR. Not now. Not with all the blood she's lost. But I do it anyway. I pound at her chest like I'm banging on the door of heaven but there's no one there. Heidi is dead. Nothing I can do will bring her back. Life slides from her beautiful face like a silk scarf falling to the floor.

I'm angry. Angry at my useless self and my useless kit for failing her. And there is a scream building in me that I want to give God, right in His face. I want to hit something. I want to tell Heidi that I never hated her, that I'm not that shallow. I want time back. Time to get to know this broken human being because, despite everything she said, I know we could have been friends — eventually. But it's too damn late now.

Outside the schoolroom the guys are continuing to fire. Ben shouts to Carlos, "Try to get around the back and get a sighting on their position. As soon as you've got a grid reference let me know — I'm gonna call in an air strike."

Carlos has gone the minute Ben stops speaking and Ben's just about to leave, too, when I grab his arm, "Lieutenant!"

"What?"

"You can't do that."

"What the hell do you mean?"

"If they use the same ordinance, Husna's evidence at the river — and maybe in the village — might be destroyed."

"We don't have any choice. Omar's buddies aren't going to give up until either we're dead or they are. We've got some evidence — it'll have to be enough."

"Then I need a Black Hawk for Heidi, too. I'm not leaving her here whatever happens." I almost choke on the words.

Ben nods. He knows. I don't have to tell him she's dead.

We scramble to a safer position behind the wall. It feels like we're there forever, but soon Carlos is calling in the grid reference. Ben stops shooting and holds his earpiece. His face is pale with stress and I find myself consumed with guilt, relief, and gratitude that he is alive. He calls his radio operator using his neck mic and tells him to request air support.

"Uh-huh, Saray, they've got us pinned down." He gives them the grid references, slowly, deliberately.

When he's done, Ben looks at me, then at Heidi. He's caked in blood and gore, which is drying now and turning the front of his camo jacket to black. I realize that I must look the same. We're both covered in Heidi's blood. "She saved my life." He tugs at his bloody jacket. "That should have been me."

We're interrupted by the thud and whistle of more incoming mortars and scatter for any available cover just as the rocks around us erupt in multiple raging explosions. Dirt and debris rain down on us — huge, skull-crushing rocks cracking and splintering as they hit the ground. I'm scared witless and have to force my muscles to respond, watching the arc of each incoming round and aiming my fire at the source. White streaks of high-caliber rounds are going in the same direction from some of Ben's guys higher up the hillside.

I can see Chip firing in short, rapid bursts from his cover. To my amazement Hammed still has the prisoner. Husna is watching Omar, and his eyes are dark with anger.

The mortar fire subsides briefly. Either we've taken out some of their positions or they are moving closer. It's unnerving. Is this it? Is this where I'm going to die? I look at Ben. His face is giving nothing away, but I wonder if he's thinking the same thing. Then I hear something I could never have imagined in a battle. From all sides, comes the sound of children's voices. They are ringing out, echoing off the steep mountainsides: *"ALLAHU AKBAR!"*

Husna stands and waves his arms in the air. His eyes are shining. "Is Young Martyrs!"

Chip pulls him down roughly, but now we're all looking at each other. I see Ben's face — and I know he's thinking the same thing. The shouting. The mortar fire subsiding . . . the Young Martyrs shouting "God is great" . . . They have been fighting for us, they've taken out an enemy mortar position, and now they are in the worst possible place they could be — right in the middle of the strike zone.

27

BEFORE I AM ABLE TO GATHER MY THOUGHTS, THE ground is shaken by three gray, delta-winged US warplanes that swoop and skim the valley walls, departing with the crack of thunder and a hail of dust. I watch the trails of vapor curl upward and disappear beyond the nearest peak. It feels like either I am deaf or all sounds of warfare have ceased.

An eerie calm descends, broken suddenly by Ben yanking me to my feet. We sprint out of the schoolroom, Ben waving to his men and yelling, "THIS WAY — NOW!" We all run at full pelt up the hill and away from the village. The roar of the jets, now distant, begins to increase in volume again. Husna screams and falls to his knees near me. I scoop him up and half run, half stumble with him sobbing in my arms. All the way, Ben runs with the radio to his ear yelling into it, "ABORT, ABORT! NONCOMBATANTS IN STRIKE ZONE! REPEAT — NC IN STRIKE ZONE! ABORT!" and all the time the thunder of the jet engines grows louder.

Then comes the dreaded sound — the hiss and rush of rockets. I glance over my shoulder and see four missiles drop from the distant wings, hang as if time has stopped, and then arc downward with frightening speed, trailing white vapor.

"COVER!" Ben yells, and we all hit the floor.

The heat of the rocket trails flash over our backs. Foolishly I lift my head to see the crushing impact. Two of the missiles strike the enemy mortar position, and the other two hit a target in the forest just beyond the poppy field almost simultaneously. The plumes of dirt, fire, and debris combine into huge fireballs, scorching our skin and clothing even from this distance. I bury my head in my arms and don't know how long I'll be able to stand the lingering, blistering heat on my neck and arms without screaming. Mercifully it lifts after a few excruciating seconds when the flames mushroom upward and the impact sites belch black, oily fumes into the sky.

Ben scrambles to his feet as the jets fly past almost close enough to touch, ignoring the shower of red-hot stones and clods of earth that drop from the sky and rattle off our helmets. We are so deafened by the explosion that we can't even hear the jets anymore. It doesn't look like they've heard Ben's call to abort and we don't know if they will come back around for another pass, so we get to our feet and race on for the high ground.

When we get there, we wait for the planes to circle back. There's nothing yet. And from the fields below, silence. But none of us thinks for a moment that it's all over. The stakes are too high. Omar's comrades must know why we're here. They'll fight to the death to stop us getting our evidence back to Kabul.

It's a moment before I realize Ben is speaking to me. His words are muffled, drowned out by the ringing in my ears. "Ellie, they're sending Apaches, too, but I may have to tell them to hold fire. Some of the kids could still be there."

I can't think about what might have happened. "They thought they were helping us."

Husna nods vigorously. He's relieved that the air attack is over — still assuming that his friends are indestructible. "Is true. They know is something wrong."

Despite the boy's enthusiasm, Ben remains cautious. "It's too soon to tell. Look, Ellie, I need you, Chip, and Gizmo to do something else for me."

"Yes, sir," Chip replies.

Gizmo nods.

"I've requested a couple of Black Hawks. One for casualties and the other so we can get Bella's papers out of here. Get to high ground — that's where the choppers will land, if they can. Take all the evidence we have and make sure it's safe.

And I want that scumbag" — he nods to Omar — "out of here, too."

A strange look flashes over Husna's face and he kicks a rock in Omar's direction. It hits the prisoner, hard, and he scowls at us. Husna moves away from me and I can tell by the way he looks back over his shoulder that he's up to something. There's no time to worry about it though.

I ask Ben, "But, Lieutenant, what about Heidi's body?"

"We'll deal with that," he tells me firmly.

I get it. He means that I won't.

"Get out of here and make sure those documents get to Macallum. He'll have to make the call about how or if we get back here to secure the cache and bring his daughter's body home. Chip, you and Gizmo need to get back to the village when you've seen Ellie and the prisoner off safely — ASAP."

I'm incensed. "You can't do that! I'm not leaving."

Chip gives me a look and I know I have overstepped the mark on two counts — forgetting his rank and questioning an order. I don't count giving away my feelings. My fear for him is written all over my face.

Ben insists, "Yes, you are, Ellie. I need the prisoner and that evidence beyond reach and you are the best person for the job. I want you to take Husna, too. It's a tactical decision."

If Ben's going to die, I want to die with him. I don't want to hear about it on some joyride back to safety. I'd do anything to stay, anything. "Why can't I come back with Chip and Gizmo?"

"Private Nielson . . ." The way he uses my rank is so final.

"So that's it? I have no choice?"

"None." A mortar thuds into the mountainside. "I've gotta go." With a brief, pained glance in my direction, Ben leaves us.

As soon as he has gone from my sight my world turns black, and I'm consumed with an emptiness so raw and so painful that I feel like my heart has been ripped, still beating, from my body. What if I never see him again? What if that's the last memory he has of me — angry? I curse my lack of self-control.

 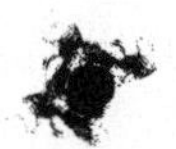

After Ben leaves I'm frustrated to discover that Husna has disappeared, too. Now I'm not even going to be able to do the one simple thing Ben asked of me. Not to mention that I won't see the boy again — even to say good-bye. I'm angry that he's just gone off, like he's done it just to hurt me. I take it out on Chip and Gizmo.

Gizmo grabs me. "Ellie, calm down!"

I don't want to calm down. I can multitask — I'll be pissed off and professional at the same time. I yank my arm out of his grasp.

Hammed delivers the prisoner to us still clamped in a headlock. "Don't worry, Ellie," he says when he sees my face, "I will look for boy, keep him safe. You go . . . go . . . make sure evidence is safe."

I have no choice. Chip and Gizmo take the prisoner between them. I keep the diary and the folder tight against my chest, and we head off up the mountain, ducking behind any cover we can find as we go. The distant thump of rotor blades sends shivers through me even though I should be thankful that help is on the way. The landscape up here is mostly low scrub, and, once we leave the few stunted pine trees behind, our only cover is the occasional dip in the rocks. We head for a ridge that looks like it might offer some protection.

Halfway up, there is a dull slapping sound and Omar yelps. He's taken a stray round in the leg. It splatters Chip's trousers with blood.

"Jeez, that was close!" Chip swears, and he and Gizmo drag our limping captive up the slope at a quickened pace.

Once we get over the ridge we find we're in the relative safety of a kind of hollow scooped out of the rocks. We run down the slope into it and Gizmo sets off a flare, backing away as it belches red smoke that clings to the ground for a few meters and then is sucked skyward in an updraft.

I can see the Black Hawk hovering not far away from the mountainside. There are two heavily armed Apaches hovering in the distance, but they don't open fire. The sounds of the battle below us intensify briefly with the thud and boom of more incoming fire. Like me, Chip and Gizmo are itching to get back, to help. But the Black Hawk doesn't move. It seems to be waiting. Only when the battle quiets briefly does it begin to come in, low and fast. Ben must have given the go-ahead.

I put the folder and the diary in my backpack, watching the Black Hawk raise a small hurricane when it touches down.

Chip and Gizmo drag our wounded prisoner to the open door and throw him inside.

Before I get in, the guys give me an awkward man-hug. I can see that neither of them wants to leave me this way.

"Stay alive," I tell them bleakly, as if they have a choice.

Chip looks at me, but he's too choked to speak. Gizmo gives me a shunt up into the helicopter, and as soon as my butt hits the floor we're airborne and lurching into a turn. The guys don't stop to watch. They just duck and run back to the action.

We rise on a cloud of dust, clearing the hollow, and I can see the steep mountain slope we have just run up, falling away until it reaches the trees. Below, the chaos of war rips the countryside apart with explosions and angry, smoking trails. I look back down the mountain toward the cave, and see a flash of blue. Aroush is there, looking up at me. Her black hair is whipping across her face in the downdraft and I just get the faintest glimmer of her eyes through it. And I know, without a shadow of doubt, it's all over for me.

28

THEN SHE IS GONE. AND IN HER PLACE A SMALL, slight shadow emerges from the cave, staggering beneath the weight of a long metal tube. It is Husna and he is carrying a rocket launcher.

He lifts the loaded weapon and brings it to bear on us. It's wobbling violently.

He thinks I've just loaded Omar onto the chopper.

I'm shaking with fear, holding my breath and willing him to think again. If I tell the gunner what I've seen, he'll kill Husna. If I don't — we're dead.

To my relief Husna seems to be having second thoughts. His head falls against the barrel of his weapon and he stands there for a moment just holding it. Then his head comes up and his expression is dead. He fumbles with something on the side of the tube.

In the same instant an alarm sounds in the cab. Husna's rocket has locked onto us. The pilot looks about wildly for the source, flicking switches and arming his weapons.

And now the gunner at the door has seen where I'm looking. He's yelling, "HOSTILE! SEVEN O'CLOCK!" and swinging his gun round.

I'm screaming, "NO!" In that moment I'm more afraid for Husna than I am for myself. But it is a waste of breath. We are about fifty or sixty meters above the ground and rising, and I can only watch in horror as the rocket launches and the recoil flips Husna onto his back. Flames shoot from the tube and the missile arcs upward with deadly accuracy. There is no time to think, no time to move, no time to prepare for death. Below us figures scatter to avoid the inevitable fireball. I was right. This is the end.

I close my eyes and in the millisecond before we are hit I feel a slight, cool hand grip mine.

Then the world around me erupts in splinters of white-hot metal and deafening sound. All light is sucked from my eyes, shadows gather around the blazing inferno. And then Aroush is by my side, holding my hand. It's as if we've become water — the angry metal rips through us, leaving little more than a ripple on the surface of my body. I'm lost in her eyes, as though the reflection of fire and carnage I see in them is all just a dream. As though I'm watching her life and mine merge. I see her crouching in the corner of the schoolroom, near a window, in the shade of an old fig tree when it is all engulfed in flame. And in the intensity of that moment, as everything around me burns and tumbles to the ground, as we are suspended between worlds, life seems to surge through every inch of us.

Below us the helicopter plummets and spins into the hillside, scattering fighters like marbles. Flames swell from the engines, and the rotor blades smash into the rocks, twisting and breaking into hot, lethal splinters. Then the fuel tank blows, and fire and smoke billow upward.

I can see Ben, shielding his face and screaming my name. My friends Chip and Gizmo, their faces blackened and haggard, staggering and sliding down the slope. Then, with a rushing, mighty wind, the shadows are sucked from my vision and everything turns white.

29

I COME TO WITH A GASP, AS THOUGH I HAVE HELD my breath for far too long.

I'm lying on my back, still strapped to what remains of my seat, halfway down the mountain. While consciousness returns, I wonder, *Have I dreamed all this?* But the heat from the burning wreck pulls the skin on the left side of my face taut and I find that I am some way from what's left of the fuselage and one twisted rotor blade. There's a pair of boots not far away, near some burning scrub. My legs are throbbing and I can't feel my feet so I have no idea if the boots are mine. There is no sign of the helicopter's other passengers. Black, acrid smoke billows all around me and as my chest tightens to squeeze out a cough, I am wracked with spasms of sheer agony. I have to move, but when I try, pain lances through my torso and my right leg. I am badly hurt.

I lift my head to look down. My leg is twisted at an impossible angle and white bone punches a bloody hole through my shin. I can do nothing but wait and hope, and as I scan the area around me for any sign of help, I notice a single bloody footprint on a boulder nearby. Frantically I strain to see through the inferno, afraid of what I might find. I try to call, but nothing comes out. Beyond the warped, smoldering remains of the helicopter's engine I can only make out a few dark stains. They lead toward a group of stunted pine trees clinging to the steep mountainside.

My eyes sting and my view is obscured by plumes of black smoke and floating shards of red-hot ash. But as I stare, I see a small shadow within the tangle of branches. I know it's Aroush.

I'm floating in and out of consciousness. Sometimes Aroush is in the trees, sometimes close, bending over me — watching. The last time I see her she is moving into the trees, glancing back over her shoulder at me. She smiles once and then she is gone. I breathe her name. She has saved me. I wonder why, how . . . if it was her way of thanking me.

Then, as the wind changes direction, I hear voices calling. My friends are looking for me. I want to shout out but I can't — it's too painful. The first face to come into focus is

Ben's. He lifts my head gently and says my name. Then I hear him shout, his voice heavy with relief, "OVER HERE! SHE'S ALIVE! God knows how, but she's alive!"

Then he falls on me and at last I feel the warmth of his kiss on my lips, and my forehead. His breath is soft on my face as he whispers, "Stay with me, honey. Everything's gonna be OK."

Chip appears in my vision, behind Ben's shoulder. He's smiling. "Bloody hell, Buffy. You had us worried."

I hear Gizmo tell Ben, "We've called for another medevac. There are two other survivors, but there's not much left of the prisoner. They won't be long now."

It's hard to imagine how anyone could come out of that wreckage alive. But it has happened. Not only that but now I can see my backpack lying on its side about four meters away. Bella's evidence is safe.

"It's a miracle," Ben says, following my gaze. "And even more of a miracle that you're in one piece." His voice is loaded with concern. "Anyone know any first aid?"

"I do," I say.

He laughs. "I'm serious."

"You can stop worrying," I tell him. "It's just a broken leg. I should splint it though."

He tries not to laugh at me. "You're not doing anything. The medevac will be here soon. Just take it easy."

I want to tell him to stop fussing, but I like it. I lift my hand to his face, not caring what Chip and Gizmo think. But they don't seem that surprised.

"Where are the Afghans?" I ask.

"On the run," Gizmo tells me. "We had them on two flanks — us and the Young Martyrs."

"God knows how, but they managed to get away from the strike zone in time," Chip adds.

When Hammed and Husna finally get to me, the boy bursts into tears. He is inconsolable. Hammed is too rough with him. He barks at the boy in Pashto, grabs him by the ears, and forces him to look at me.

I reach out and take his hand. "It's OK," I say weakly, "I understand. I saw what happened."

"Why you on chopper, Ellie? Why?" the boy sobs. "I thinking you coming back. Why you get in?"

I stop him. "It's over, Husna. It's all over," but really I know that it's not. I'm beginning to realize that in war nothing ever ends happily ever after. Especially not for the kids. I'm guessing all you can hope for is to live long enough to make sense of it. I pull at his limp hand and, as he sits beside me, I manage to draw him closer and ruffle his hair. At last the tension drains from his body. When I look up I'm amazed to see that Hammed's eyes meet mine and he does not look away.

I catch some movement near the trees where I last saw Aroush. A ragged bunch of kids, their clothes shabby and torn, emerge from the shadows.

Husna gets to his feet and waves.

One of them waves back and throws his gun on the floor. I wonder if somehow Aroush has made them understand that they do not need to fight anymore, that their war is over. More and more emerge. There must be about fifteen of them, disheveled and as thin as rakes.

"Hey, I thought you said there were hundreds of Young Martyrs," I say to Husna accusingly.

He gives us one of his trademark shrugs, and we all laugh.

"What do you think will happen to them?" I ask Ben.

"I'm not sure" — he smiles — "but I'm guessing it will be on their terms. Maybe we can pull some strings, keep them together, eh, Hammed?"

"No orphanage in Helmand," Hammed mutters, "but plenty community spirit."

Ben leaves to deal with the cleanup operation, taking Bella's evidence with him. I know it's stupid to hope he would see me off, he has more important things to do, but I can't help it. I have no idea when I'm ever going to see him again. He'll stay in Helmand on operations and when they've fixed my leg up I'll probably be shipped straight back home. It could be months before I get back to duty, by which time he will be long gone. Who knows what his next mission will be, or even if he'll come out of it alive? Why didn't I ask him for a number, address, e-mail — anything? Why? Because I'm in a sodding war zone, that's why. And I'm a soldier. And this wasn't supposed to happen.

Chip and Gizmo watch the paramedics put me on the

chopper with the other two crash survivors, the pilot and the gunner.

The pilot's face is lacerated and bloody, but he's conscious and he can still see, thank God. The paramedics have him strapped to a stretcher in a head brace; they're not taking any chances. The gunner is on another stretcher. He seems to be sliding in and out of consciousness. His left arm is broken in several places and he has shrapnel wounds all up that side of his torso. As for me, my leg has been splinted, even though the bone is still poking out. Classic field treatment. It's not going purple, though, so the circulation is still OK. It still amazes me that any of us should have walked away from this, that somehow we're all going to live.

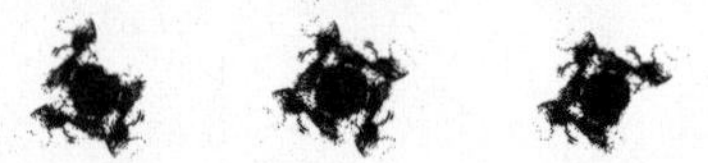

When we get to the field hospital at Camp Bastion it's a haze of poking, prodding, and X-rays before they rush me into the operating room. Next thing I know I'm waking up in a ward bed with my leg throbbing and suspended in a traction pulley.

I count myself lucky when I scan the other beds. Opposite is an unconscious guy with two bandaged stumps for arms. On my right, someone on his side, also out of it. No idea what his injuries are. The others have the curtains pulled and the room is filled with pulsing, bleeping, and humming machines. And I get the tang of blood and medical alcohol in the back of my throat every time I take a breath. I feel as if half of me is still lying somewhere out there in the mountains of Helmand. I've never felt so lost and alone, and I have nothing to do but lie here and think.

On my second day, one of the nurses notices my mood. She takes pity on me and lends me her radio so I can listen to the British Forces radio station. That's where I hear that an Afghan minister has been arrested trying to flee the capital, but there are no more details as to who it is yet or why. Other than to say that joint operations between interior forces and the coalition have been temporarily suspended.

Every time I tune in to the news after that, all I get for my trouble is frustration. Nothing more. Nothing! But the arrest is down to Bella's evidence — I know it.

30

AFTER FOUR DAYS I'M TOLD THAT THERE IS A FLIGHT back to England for me and the guy with no arms. It leaves at midday and when I lift myself onto my elbows to check the time it's already ten o'clock. They're sending me to some new hospital in Birmingham and I'm never going to see Ben again. I flop back onto my pillow and close my eyes in despair.

It is a slight change in air quality — a whisper of a breath — that makes me open them again, but no one's there. Just a familiar scent, at once earthy and fragrant. Then I see the curtain move.

My heart leaps when Ben steps out from behind it, all dusty from the road, a broad smile spreading across his face.

He's hiding something behind his back. He bends to kiss my lips before I can say anything else. When we part his eyes are sparkling.

"Hi," he says quietly.

There is so much to say, to ask, but when I open my mouth I find myself babbling, "Where did you go? I was so worried. I didn't think I was ever going to see you again. I thought I'd go home and never —"

He puts a finger to my lips and there is no doubt in his voice. "I would have found you."

While he straightens up I realize that I haven't thought about getting better until this moment. Now I just want to get on my feet again.

"I've brought you something," he says, and pulls a roll of paper from behind his back. "You have no idea what it took to get ahold of this. It's the first copy to land out here."

I take it from him and unroll it. It's the *Washington Post*, the newspaper Bella Macallum worked for. The banner headline reads "WARLORD EXPOSED," with a picture of a man, mobbed by the press, being shoved into the backseat of a big black car. Beneath that a subheading: "*Post* reporter Bella Macallum found in Helmand." There is a color picture of her in a plain white blouse on the front page. Her piercing green eyes, the fine features, the raven-black hair — they're all Aroush.

"Look at the center pages," Ben tells me, and he sits on the bed to watch as I open it. It's a two-page spread with copies of parts of the documents we found in the cave, including some extracts from her diary.

WARLORD

February 9: *Stonewalled in Kabul. My contact, "D," can't talk yet — if my suspicions are right, who can blame him for being cautious?*

February 11: *My cell phone is definitely being tapped. I'm having to borrow from random Westerners I meet. They're so shocked to see an American in a burka but I like it — it keeps me anonymous. Dad is going to start his duties as the new commander of US forces in Afghanistan in a couple of weeks. I wonder if he'd see me if I tried to find him? Maybe we could forget our differences. All the foreigners in town are talking about whether or not the Taliban will be brought into talks with the Afghan government before Western forces leave the country for good.*

February 15: *Almost gave up waiting for "D" but he finally met me by the bus stop — I thought I was being abducted when he grabbed my arm. He's got evidence, but he is wary. All he would tell me was that I am right — one of the government ministers is definitely a Taliban warlord. The last thing the traitor wants is for the coalition to open talks with the Taliban because then he will be exposed and everyone will know he's been using his government position to get rich. There are billions of dollars to be made in Saray. The mountains around our village are full of lithium. It's used in the majority of the world's batteries, even in my Mac. I had no idea. The rogue*

EXPOSED

minister is offering to sell mining rights to the highest bidder. "D" says that the Taliban who are making us farm opium poppies in Saray are loyal to the minister. He says Taliban are even in units of the Afghan security force, and that the minister has been using his influence and American money to buy arms for them. They're hiding a cache of weapons up here somewhere. I'm going to try and find it. "D" will send documentary evidence in the next week or so if he can.

MARCH 9: *It's been three weeks now. I've been waiting here in Saray and still there is nothing from "D." Now time really has run out for us thanks to my brave, crazy husband. I'm so mad at Jahadar. Why now? He got the village together and ran the Taliban out of town — he's ruined everything and we had a huge fight about it. I should be proud of him, but he's put us all in danger. I've asked Mullah Behzad to take what little I know to Dad — today.*

MARCH 10: *Finally! The evidence I need is here. It's everything I hoped but too late. Jahadar organized the whole village yesterday to prepare for when the Taliban return, and I don't want to leave Saray without him.*

Post reporter Bella Macallum found in Helm

It's the last entry.

"I knew it!" I say. "Bella's suspect in the Afghan government wanted her and the villagers wiped out to clear the way for mining, and he was able to use Taliban, Afghan security forces, and US drones to do it. Somehow he found out that she was onto him. The Taliban warlord in the Afghan cabinet is the guy at the top, isn't it, Ben? The interior minister, Zalmai Khan."

He nods. "There was a press embargo because Macallum was talking with the government about Taliban involvement in a peace conference, but they released the story yesterday. Khan wanted Bella dead, along with all the evidence and anybody who may have heard about it. He must have hit the roof when the Young Martyrs turned up and spoiled it all for him."

We turn our attention back to the article. There are a number of grainy, long-lens shots of Zalmai Khan talking with heavily armed insurgents in the mountains. The article details the repeated requests Khan made for arms for his elite Afghan security forces, and how Bella discovered he was smuggling Russian weapons across the border from Pakistan, too. There are even numbers for some of the arms shipments. No doubt one or two will match boxes we found in the cave.

Ben folds the paper. "She was a brave woman. Too dangerous for Khan to leave to chance. They must have traced her through 'D.' Bet he's dead, too. The Taliban who were making Bella's village produce opium were loyal to Khan. They were in league with the renegade Afghan security unit who ambushed us in Husna's village and kidnapped Bella and her husband before the village was bombed."

We sit in silence.

"Aroush," Ben says eventually. "You saw her?"

I nod.

"I've told Macallum she's dead," he says, looking at me evenly.

Under the circumstances, it's probably the best thing he could have said. I'm not sure I'll ever get my head around Aroush — all I know is I'll never see her again.

"What about Husna?" I ask. "What's going to happen to him?"

"Hammed has got the villagers of Darzab looking after him and the Young Martyrs. And he's trying to trace the girls from the village so they can be reunited. I think he's also hoping to get statements from all the kids so he can present it to the court when Khan and his men go to trial. He wants justice for Farshad and the Young Martyrs . . ."

He leans over and kisses me again, then stands. "I have to go."

"How will I find you?"

He laughs. "You won't — I'm Special Forces, remember?"

"Don't joke."

"Elinor, when this tour is over I'll make it *my* mission to find *you*." He smiles. "And I've never failed a mission yet."

It's hard to watch the doors swing shut behind him, but as I lose sight of him I know without a shadow of a doubt that he will be true to his word. He will find me.

All I can do now is lie here, waiting for my flight to England and thinking of the day I arrived. I thought I'd be saving lives, winning hearts and minds — but who was I kidding? I've saved one life only to see it lost again. I've watched a child die, and I've experienced fear like no other. I should feel hopeless, dejected, but for some reason I don't. And then, as I think about this place and everyone I've met here, I realize why. It's the people. They fill me with hope. Real, burning hope.

AUTHOR'S NOTE

It's not easy to trace the process that ultimately inspired me to write my novel *Torn*. I've never been to Afghanistan, and I've never fought in a war, but I have met people who have made me think deeply about both — children dealing with the aftermath of the Romanian Revolution in Eastern Europe, and soldiers who have fought in Iraq, Afghanistan, or both. And, of course, there is that famous photograph from the cover of the June 1985 issue of *National Geographic* magazine — the one of the Afghan refugee girl with the shell-shocked, piercing green eyes. All these things compelled me to think about what war is, who gets caught up in it, and how it affects them day by day — in their living and their dying.

REVOLUTIONARY ROMANIA

I remember standing in the town square in Timisoara, Romania. It was the end of December 1989 and just weeks before, in what was then East Germany, groups of protestors had begun to tear down the Berlin Wall. After more than forty years of Communist rule, the central European nations of the so-called Eastern Bloc were fighting to reclaim their independence from the Soviet Union. But these popular uprisings were rife with danger, and the revolutionaries had to organize in secret. Earlier in the year I had been asked by a Christian charity, Jubilee Campaign, to smuggle clothes, food, and bibles to a church group in Timisoara before traveling on to a Baptist seminary in Bucharest. The churches were leading the movement for change in many of the Communist countries and needed support. Following the arrest of Assistant Pastor László Tőkés in Timisoara and while we were planning the trip, Romania began staging a revolution of its own. Now our mission was to focus on getting food and urgent medical supplies in as quickly as possible and to check out reports that were emerging about appalling conditions in the country's orphanages. Like thousands of others, I was a witness.

The air in the square was freezing cold and smelled of wet wool. All around us the snow had been trampled into a brown sludge by throngs of people stamping their feet and rubbing their hands. They were all dressed in dark, heavy coats, moving like shadows, wreathed in fingers of steam that rose from damp paving slabs that had been warmed by a few hours of winter sun. Relatives of all ages had gathered in the town square to pay respect to their dead. Some of them quietly placed pictures of their loved ones against lampposts and lit candles. Some knelt and placed flowers. Some wept. And some just stood there in silent disbelief, looking at the sky. Here, on the seventeenth of December, after Pastor Tőkés's arrest, security forces had opened fire on crowds of unarmed demonstrators, killing ninety-seven people and injuring many others. The event quickly became one of the flashpoints of the entire revolution, and every day people came to the square to honor the fallen.

Along with my friends Steve and Paul, I was in Timisoara to drop off donations at the local Baptist church for distribution. Before we could set off in search of the minister's house, a boy of about ten or twelve, wearing two heavy coats and a thick woollen hat, virtually pulled the three of us from our big Mercedes truck. The boy could only speak a few words of English and we could not speak any Romanian, so he used gestures instead.

"Chocolate?" he asked meaningfully.

We laughed and gave him some Cadbury bars in the shadow of the truck, to keep from getting mobbed by marauding children — as we'd already been on our way there.

The boy smiled. He waved urgently at us to follow him, and led us to the square.

It was the site of the massacre a week or two ago, we knew that much. But to our new friend it wasn't some international news flash;

it was where people he knew had been shot dead. And he wanted to tell us all about it. He wanted us to go home and tell the world.

With an earnest, deathly gray look on his face he took us to a doorway and pointed out the places where bullets had hammered chunks out of the bricks. A line of small, neat holes ran through the reinforced glass panels in the door.

The boy made his arms into a machine gun and shouted, "*Rat-a-tat-tat!*" through a mouthful of chocolate. Then he pulled us from the battered doorway to a few of the makeshift shrines. He pointed to the photographs — to the ghostly, still faces of friends who'd been cut down. One picture was of an old woman — I think it may have been his grandmother. Other pictures were of the young — many of them much too young.

As this nameless boy led us through the square, I wondered: Did he even have any family left? Was he fending for himself or depending upon the kindness of strangers now? I never found out. But the uneasiness I felt when we left him has remained with me ever since. It was dark when we departed Timisoara. Pitch-black. The streetlights didn't work because the power stations weren't operating, and the roads were like sheets of ice. I don't remember how we found the house of the Baptist minister who was our contact, but I do remember the first thing he and his two teenage sons showed us: their homemade video from earlier that day of the two boys lifting the pale, bloated bodies of the massacre victims out of the pit they had been thrown into.

"This is my aunt," one of the boys told us as we watched the body flop onto its back.

My friends and I had a lot to think about as we journeyed onward through Transylvania to Bucharest, driving through small Romanian towns with a single main road, often guarded at both ends by wary soldiers. Several times we ran the armed checkpoints in our truck because the Red Cross had advised us not to stop for people with guns. In fact, they had told us not to travel at night at all, but, determined to deliver our food and medical supplies, we were pressed for time. There was still the sound of shooting at night, echoing through empty streets, and when at last we got to the capital, there were more graves and caskets. The red-faced principal of the seminary told us that when the dictator Ceausescu's huge, obscene palace had been stormed, it was the children who led the charge up the steps. I've never been able to verify the truth of that. But I have no reason to believe he was lying.

"The adults were much too frightened to start it," he told us in halting English. It took the brave, reckless abandon of youth to instigate the surge that overwhelmed the guards and that would suddenly bring down a regime that had murdered countless innocents and brutally oppressed its own people.

Since my time as a volunteer in Romania more than twenty years ago, I have thought often of the boy we met in the town square, and wondered a lot about young people and war. What happens to kids when they lose their friends and family in a conflict? How do they survive? Meeting those young people in Romania is probably why Husna and the Young Martyrs are so close to my heart in *Torn*.

THE GIRL WITH THE GREEN EYES

The image of the mysterious Afghan girl, Aroush, haunted my thoughts from the first minute I sat down to write this story. In 2010, an exhibition of the photographs of Steve McCurry came to my hometown of Birmingham, England. His most famous photo is the startling image of Sharbat Gula, which had first appeared on the cover of *National Geographic* in June 1985. It's the most recognized photograph in the history of the magazine, and it's not hard to see why. Sharbat's piercing sea-green eyes have seen things no one should ever see. In the early 1980s, her parents were killed in a Soviet air strike on her hometown, and she fled Afghanistan with

ACKNOWLEDGMENTS

Like Elinor, I went into this process as an individual and came out of it as part of a team. I found that to get somewhere, you first need to get your boots on, find your fellow squaddies, and set out. Then it is a good idea to listen to those who can give you some guidance along the way. So thanks to Barry, Rachel H., Laura, and all the Chicken House readers for believing that there was any point in getting off the sofa and setting out in the first place. Special thanks to Imogen Cooper and Rachel Leyshon for their inspired editorial input, and to Miranda Baker for going over everything with a fine-toothed comb.

For the American edition I'm in debt to Siobhán McGowan and Rachel Kuck, who ensured that my characters know their pants from their trousers and don't set off on a day's march without a pair of tightly laced combats.

Thanks also to Colin Vallance for reading *Torn* too many times to mention, giving so much valuable input and always finding fresh ways of looking at it. To Stephen Massey for some great practical advice and insights — all those hours spent playing *Call of Duty* weren't wasted, then — Anna Smith for taking a break from slapping emulsion on walls to offer input on titles and taglines, and Josh Wunderlich for introducing me to some great music, having a keen eye for detail, and being my YA insider.

Thank you to my beautiful wife, Debi, who has kept me sane throughout and who can encourage, inspire, and edit, all while juggling a business, studies, and a family — without even breaking into a sweat.

Final thanks go to Ebony the cat for keeping me awake by biting my feet when the coffee didn't work anymore and to Harvey — yes, you can have that walk now but don't you dare chew up the mail from now on.

about the Afghan conflict and the army world he loved. Like Elinor, he had been a medic with the commandos. But now, in civilian life, he was a recovering amputee. I was struck by his optimism and how he faced his new battles with amazing inner strength, humor, and dignity. I hope some of that spirit also inhabits *Torn*.

As I write this, the first day of the 2012 London Paralympics is underway, with the numbers of the American and British teams swollen by war heroes, broken but unbowed, determined to fight back. The athletes' stories are inspirational. Martine Wright, a survivor of the July 7, 2005, London bombings, plays floor volleyball. Derek Derenalagi, at first pronounced dead after his vehicle hit an IED, throws discus and javelin. Mohammad Fahim Rahimi, the lone Afghan weightlifter representing his country, trod on a landmine as a child. These athletes are just the tip of the iceberg. In every walk of life there are people who have been affected by conflict. I can only hope that, in some small way, *Torn* honors these military and civilian victims of war and their incomprehensible sacrifices.

The thought that Elinor could be like them — a healer, a soldier dedicated to saving lives rather than taking them — really appealed to me. My wife and I run an emergency supplies business where we provide just the kinds of materials that a medic like Elinor would use. At counter terrorism, police, and emergency services events, we often meet with and talk to soldiers between tours of duty. Many of them have spoken to me about their experiences in Iraq, Kuwait, and Afghanistan, and their stories helped me to build up a picture of life on the front lines. Even though Afghanistan is such a faraway place, the fallout from the conflict there affects us, too. Birmingham, England, where I live, has long been one of the first places coalition service personnel arrive after they have been badly injured in combat. When visiting the world-renowned trauma unit in the Queen Elizabeth Hospital, I discovered that it was always full of soldiers in uniform, and I wondered who they were visiting, what their stories were. A military hospital emergency room is no place to tell people you are researching a novel about war, or to ask them about their personal experiences. So while writing, videos and documentaries became my eyes and ears into Ellie's world. With increasing admiration, I watched how our armed forces try day after day to make a difference in Afghanistan — how they get up each morning prepared to lay down their lives in service for their country. And then they face a nebulous war zone, one with no clear beginning or end. The front line in Afghanistan is not marked with trenches or barbed wire. Out there, the front line finds you, whether you're a Navy SEAL like Ben or a medic like Elinor.

Shortly after finishing *Torn*, I met the remarkable Bravo 22 Company: Its members include soldiers maimed by Improvised Explosive Devices in Afghanistan and Iraq. Their stories had been adapted into a play that these same injured soldiers performed to critical acclaim in London. The lead, a Canadian soldier named Cassidy Little, was pleased to hear that I'd written a novel her siblings. By the time Steve McCurry came across her, she was living in a Pakistani refugee camp: That's where he photographed his now-iconic portrait. Years later, Sharbat was traced down using a biometric scan of those amazing eyes — quite poetic! But the most powerful thing about that image for me was in *not knowing* what lay behind them. Even though I had never read the magazine article, this famous image was etched into my memory. Interestingly, in *Torn*, the character of Aroush was also caught up in an air strike, and the other girls from the story's fictional village fled to Pakistan — all before I ever knew that this was what had happened to Sharbat Gula in real life.

BRAVO 22

Civilians like Sharbat or the nameless Romanian boy are not the only victims of war, of course. Like most people in Britain and the United States, I have watched news bulletins night after night that show the flag-draped coffins of our brave service men and women making their last journey home from Iraq or Afghanistan. I can only imagine what life and death in a war zone must have been like for them.

So many young adults have died for their country in the war on terror. It struck me that their stories are not often told, and I decided that I wanted to tell one — through the eyes of a young adult just like US Army Specialist Monica Lin Brown or British Lance Corporal Kylie Watson. Brown, I discovered, was the first American woman to receive the Silver Star in Afghanistan. At the age of eighteen, she saved the lives of her fellow soldiers after the detonation of a roadside bomb, shielding the wounded against incoming mortar fire with her own body. Watson won the Military Cross at age twenty-three for running to the aid of two Afghan army casualties in exposed positions, attempting to resuscitate one of them as bullets smashed into the dust around her for twenty minutes.